Why did everyone Kim wondered. He who made a lot of rude jo even as she told herself how terrible she couldn't get the image of his warm brown eyes out of her mind. When they had bumped into each other at Mrs. Garcia's, his eyes were the first thing she saw, and they had burned themselves into her memory.

"I *hate* him," she mumbled out loud, trying to sound convinced. If only she could get herself to believe it.

Here is a selection of
Bantam Sweet Dreams Romances
Ask your bookseller for the books you have missed

# Here's My Heart

Stefanie Curtis

**BANTAM BOOKS**
TORONTO • NEW YORK • LONDON • SYDNEY • AUCKLAND

RL 6, IL age 11 and up

HERE'S MY HEART
*A Bantam Book/March 1988*

*Sweet Dreams and its associated logo are registered trademarks of
Bantam Books, Inc. Registered in U.S. Patent and Trademark
Office and elsewhere.*

*Cover photo by Pat Hill.*

ISBN 0-553-26566-0

Bantam Books are published by Bantam Books, Inc. Its trademark,
consisting of the words "Bantam Books" and the portrayal of a
rooster, is Registered in U.S. Patent and Trademark Office and in
other countries. Marca Registrada. Bantam Books, Inc., 666 Fifth
Avenue, New York, New York 10103.

Printed and bound in Great Britain by
Cox & Wyman Ltd.; Reading

*For Scott Banfield*

# Chapter One

Kim Sommers sat on her bed, tapping her foot impatiently. She was going to burst if she didn't tell someone her news right away. *What's taking Maria and Joan so long?* she wondered.

She stood up and looked in the mirror on her closet door, carefully examining the clothes she had decided to wear to the basketball game that night. Her loose purple cotton sweater looked great with her off-white jeans. It was Kim's favorite outfit. But she wondered if wearing her long blond hair in a single braid was such a good idea. Maybe it would look better loose.

She was thinking about undoing the braid when Kim heard a car pull into the driveway. With a leap she was at her window, looking down at the driveway and Joan's beat-up Volks-wagen. *Finally,* she thought. *They're here.*

Kim left her hair in the braid and ran down-stairs to greet her friends. A minute later Kim and her two best friends Maria and Joan were back in Kim's bedroom. Maria and Joan both looked as though they were about to die of curiosity.

"OK," Joan blurted out, sitting cross-legged on Kim's floor and looking up at her expec-tantly. "What's the big secret?"

Maria tried to guess. "Did somebody ask you out?" she asked. "I know, it's somebody we all know but would never suspect. Someone like—" Maria stopped short, realizing that she was wrong from the look on Kim's face.

"No!" Kim said, giving Maria a withering look. "That's not it at all," she said, wishing it *were* her secret.

"There's more to life than boys," Joan reminded Maria.

Maria looked a little embarrassed. "You bought a new outfit?" she asked feebly, still trying to guess.

"Wrong again," Kim said. She sat down on the rocker next to her dresser and paused for dramatic effect.

"Tell us, will you?" Joan urged.

Finally Kim couldn't wait any longer. "Vicki's getting married," she announced.

"Vicki, as in your sister Vicki?" Joan asked, her eyes wide with shock.

Kim nodded. She could hardly believe it herself. Vicki was her only sister. "In five weeks," she added.

"*Five weeks*?" Maria exclaimed.

"Mmm-hmm. On Valentine's Day, no less," Kim said, smiling.

"That's so corny," Joan remarked skeptically.

"I think it's kind of sweet," Maria said, looking dreamy eyed. "She's marrying Max, isn't she?"

"Who else?" Kim replied. Vicki and Max had been going together for almost five years.

"Isn't Vicki a little young to be doing something so—drastic?" Joan asked.

"She's twenty," Kim replied. "I guess that's old enough." But Kim didn't really think it was. There was only a five-year difference in their ages, and Kim knew she wouldn't be ready for such a big step at Vicki's age.

"When did you find out?" Joan asked, interrupting Kim's thoughts.

"Right before dinner. Max came over and talked to my dad. Then my dad called us all in and told us. You guys should have seen it. My mom even cried."

Maria, who was still standing up, pulled a pillow over to the wall beneath Kim's life-size Springsteen poster and plunked herself down. "Details, details," she demanded, leaning forward.

Kim explained the circumstances. Max had decided to transfer across the country to Middlebury College in Vermont because of some courses that would be offered there starting the next summer. After a lot of discussion, Max and Vicki had decided to get married instead of being separated. Max and Vicki were taking that semester off, and they would spend the time between the wedding and the start of their new classes getting settled in Vermont. Kim was just about to explain how and where Max had proposed when she realized she had forgotten one of the most important pieces of news.

"Oh, and you know what else?" she asked with a big grin. "I'm going to be one of the bridesmaids!"

The news didn't thrill Joan as much as it did Maria. "How terrific!" Maria practically shouted. "Have you seen your dress yet? What's it like?"

"I don't know what it's like. Vicki hasn't picked them out yet," Kim said. Her nervousness showed in her voice. As excited as she was, she was a little worried about the bridesmaids' gowns. "I'm so tall," she explained. "I don't look good in those ruffled, fussy dresses most bridesmaids wear."

"Oh, come on, Kim," Maria said wearily. They had been through this many times. "You're not *that* tall."

"I'm the third tallest girl in our class," Kim replied defiantly.

"Well, at least you're not *the* tallest. Or even the second tallest," Maria said reasonably. "Who are the other bridesmaids?" she asked in a lighter tone, trying to change the subject.

"One of Vicki's sorority sisters and her best friend, Elaine. Elaine's the maid of honor."

"Really," Maria replied, sounding a little surprised. "If Vicki were my sister, I'd be furious if she didn't ask me to be her maid of honor."

"It's OK," Kim explained, standing up and moving to her bed. She absently smoothed a wrinkle out on her bedspread and then flopped down on her stomach. She continued, "Vicki said she really wanted to ask me, but since Elaine is engaged to the best man, Vicki thought it would be nicer if they were paired together."

"I guess she's right," Maria agreed. "Do you mind?"

"No, I really don't," Kim replied honestly. "I'm just excited to be in the wedding. I've never been a bridesmaid before."

5

"Where's it going to be held?" Joan asked, trying to sound interested. It was obvious that she didn't particularly care who was maid of honor or where the wedding was. Restlessly, Joan pulled on the fraying threads that edged a hole in her sneaker.

"In the garden at the Palms Hotel," Kim replied.

"How romantic!" Maria exclaimed. She looked over at Joan, whose attention had wandered. "Isn't it, Joanie?" Maria prompted her.

"I guess," Joan replied vaguely. It was no secret that Joan wasn't all that interested in boys or romance—at least as far as anyone could tell. All Joan seemed to care about was sports.

"Do you guys ever wonder what your own wedding day will be like?" Maria asked, with a smile on her face. "You know, where it will be?"

"I'm going to get married on the beach at sunrise," Kim said immediately. She had thought about it many times before.

Maria looked over to Joan. "I'd like to get married on top of an elephant," Joan volunteered, giving her friends a mischievous smile.

"Come on, Joanie. Be serious," Maria groaned.

"I *am* serious. I love elephants!"

"That's not the point," Maria said. "Be honest."

"I've never really thought about it," Joan admitted. "I guess I'll wait to see what Vicki's wedding is like and then decide. It sounds so neat."

"Well, you're both invited," Kim broke in. "I've already asked Vicki, and she said to make sure you both know that she wants you to be there."

It wasn't surprising that Vicki would invite Maria and Joan. They had all grown up on the same street, and the three younger girls had been best friends forever. Their mothers were still close friends, even though Maria and Joan had since moved to different neighborhoods.

"I can't wait," Maria said, hugging her knees to her chest. "Who else is going to be in the wedding party? Any cute ushers?" she asked playfully, her brown eyes twinkling.

"The ushers are mostly Max's friends from college," Kim said. "You do know who one of them is, though."

"Oh, who?"

"Rick Stone," Kim said after a slight pause.

"No kidding!" Maria made it sound as though it were an unbelievable stroke of good luck. "He's so cute."

Kim shook her head slowly. "I don't like him very much," she confessed, somehow embarrassed about admitting it. Rick Stone had recently transferred to Santa Barbara High. He had arrived a couple of months earlier. Rick was dark and handsome and seemed to have everything going for him. Kim knew she had no actual reason not to like him, but he seemed smug to her.

The first time she had seen him he was in the hall in school with her friend Denise. Denise knew him slightly, and they had stopped to talk to him for a minute. Denise was obviously crazy about him. She hadn't bothered to introduce them, and Rick hadn't seemed to care whether or not he knew who Kim was.

Rick had finally given Kim a disinterested glance that made her feel as though he were looking right through her. Kim thought Denise wasn't being polite, but she decided that it didn't matter to her. She was sure Rick was an arrogant snob, and that was that. Since then, she still hadn't been formally introduced to him, but she continued to hold to her first impression of him.

"You've got to like Rick," Maria continued with a teasing look in her eyes. "When Vicki and Max are married, he'll be your brother-in-law or something, won't he?"

"No, he won't," Kim said flatly. "He isn't Max's brother."

"He's not?" Joan asked, obviously surprised. Sometimes Joan was hopelessly ignorant about the boys at school.

"No," Kim explained, "Max and Rick are cousins. After Rick's parents died, Max's family took him in. That's why he just came to Santa Barbara. So I don't think he'll become any relation to me at all," she said to Maria.

"Well, all the better," Maria replied, tossing her black hair over her shoulder. "This is the perfect opportunity for you. I think he's kind of cute."

"*I* think he's conceited," Kim said. "He acts like he's the most important person in the world."

"Who cares, anyway?" Joan interrupted, bringing the discussion to a close. "We're going to be late for the game if we don't get going."

Maria laughed. "Oh, Joanie," she said, "when are we ever going to get you interested in the important things in life?"

"Like boys?" Joan asked, laughing, too.

"Yes, boys!" Maria retorted.

Joan shot her an uneasy grin. "Probably never," she said, glancing at her watch. "Now come on. We're going to be late if we don't leave right now."

Joan's apparent lack of interest in boys was a running joke among them. Everyone must be looking for that special person, Kim thought. Even Joan. Despite what Joan said, Kim thought her attitude was all a big act.

They left Kim's house and stepped outside into the California night. Even though it was January, the air was warm. Kim threw the light jacket she'd brought along onto the backseat of Joan's Volkswagen and then climbed in herself.

Joan's car had seen better days. It was once her brother's, but he had bought a new car and donated the old one to Joan when she had gotten her driver's license the month before. Joan was the only one of them who had a license, not to mention a car, and Maria and Kim were finally getting used to the idea of not having to ask their parents for rides everywhere. Being able to go places by themselves seemed so grown-up. As a joke, Joan had named the car Veronica Volkswagen, but what was even funnier was the way Joan talked to the car. It was almost as if the car were her pet or something.

As soon as she got in, Joan scratched the ceiling of the car, as though she were scratching behind a dog's ear. "Hello, Veronica," she chirped. "Do you want to go with us to the basketball game?" Kim and Maria cracked up.

Joan searched in her purse for her keys. When she found them, she turned to her friends. "Seat belts fastened?" she asked. Determined to be a good driver, Joan was being super-cautious.

"Seat belts fastened," Maria and Kim assured her.

Veronica started up with a cough when Joan turned the key. "Here we go," Joan said uncertainly. Looking over her shoulder, she slowly backed out of the driveway and into the street, just missing a garbage can that was sitting near the curb.

"That was a close one," Maria said, teasing her friend.

"Don't worry," Kim said in a calm voice. "You're doing great, Joanie." It had taken a lot of talking to persuade her parents to let her ride with Joan, and she wanted to do everything possible to encourage her friend to drive safely.

They took the long route to the high school, avoiding the freeway because Joan didn't feel comfortable driving on it yet. Once Joan seemed sure of herself and in control, Kim relaxed and leaned forward to talk to Maria.

"How's Peter doing?" she asked. Peter Miles, one of the stars of the basketball team, was Maria's boyfriend.

"He's doing really well," Maria replied. She looked as though she were about to yawn. "He made the all-city team last week."

"Really?" Joan said eagerly. She sounded a lot more impressed than she had about Vicki's upcoming wedding.

"Mmm-hmm," Maria said, inspecting her nails. Even though Peter was one of the most popular boys in school, Maria always acted very casual about their relationship. Kim sometimes thought her low-key attitude might be the secret to Maria's success with boys.

"Is he meeting us—I mean you—after the game?" Joan asked.

"Uh-huh. At Emilio's," Maria replied, naming the popular pizza parlor where kids in their crowd usually hung out. Her attention seemed to be focused somewhere else, though. "What's this?" she asked, pulling a paper bag out from where it had been wedged between the two front seats.

"That's just some dry grout. I use it for the parallel bars," Joan replied. Joan was one of the stars of the school gymnastic team. "It keeps my hands from slipping."

"Only you would have a bag of grout in your car," Maria said to Joan, rolling her eyes. Kim grinned. It was typical of Joanie.

The school parking lot was full when they got to the gym, so they drove down a side street to look for a place to park. Kim spotted one first, a smallish space under a large palm tree. Joan groaned when she saw it. "I hate parallel parking," she said with a sigh. "I nearly flunked the driving test because of it."

Still, she managed to maneuver the car into the spot after only three tries. Maria and Kim got out and marveled at how close Joan had gotten to the curb. Then Joan patted Veronica's hood and told her to wait there and they'd be back soon.

When the girls got inside, they found that the gym was packed, and the only empty seats they saw were very high up in the back of the bleachers. The cheerleaders had just started a cheer, and the audience was clapping and stomping in rhythm. The bleachers vibrated as the girls climbed to the back. Just as they reached the empty seats and sat down, the cheer ended and the National Anthem rang out from the loudspeaker. They stood up again.

As the music played, Kim's mind wandered. She looked around the crowded gym, searching the faces for some sign—some indication that *he* was there. She imagined that somewhere in the huge crowd around her was the boy she'd fall in love with someday. They hadn't found each other yet, but she pretended he was there, somewhere, looking for her. Every time she had been in a large crowd lately, she had wondered the same thing. *Is he here? What's he wearing tonight? Is he thinking of me?*

Kim's thoughts returned to the present when

the National Anthem ended. Everyone sat down. Out of the corner of her eye, Kim saw some people moving toward them, heading for the empty seats to her left. She didn't pay much attention to them, but it did register that they were three boys. When the boy in the middle tried to make his way past her, he stepped down solidly on her right foot. It seemed like an accident, but she glared at him in pain and surprise.

The toe masher turned out to be Whiz O'Neal, one of the most obnoxious guys in the whole school. He had earned his bizarre nickname by being the school's champion runner. And just then, Whiz certainly didn't look as if he were in a very generous mood. He glared back at her.

Maria, who had seen the whole thing, stared at Whiz angrily. "Aren't you going to apologize?" she demanded.

"I'm sorry," Whiz said to Kim, not sounding apologetic at all. "I'm sorry that I stepped on your *big feet!*"

Whiz then continued down the row, leaving Kim flushed with embarrassment. The boy behind Whiz stepped carefully around her, before turning to look at her. To Kim's utter dismay, it was none other than Rick Stone, Max's cousin. After a long, curious look, Rick sat down with his friends three seats away from her.

Kim rubbed her toe, then stole a peek at Rick. He was wearing baggy tan pants and a dark blue pullover. His thick brown hair was curly and fairly long. He leaned over to Whiz to say something, and Kim heard him ask who she was.

"Her?" Whiz announced, loud enough for everyone in the back to hear. "That's Kim *Kong*." He broke up laughing at his own bad joke. Rick started laughing, too. Kim wanted to crawl under the bleachers and die.

Maria nudged her on the arm to get her attention. *Ignore them*, she mouthed silently and turned to watch the game. The players were running out onto the court, and just then, Peter appeared. Maria nudged Kim again. "Go, Peter!" she yelled and looked at Kim expectantly.

"Yay Peter," Kim echoed feebly. Her heart wasn't in it, though. She was so upset she was almost shaking. *Kim Kong*, she thought. *Is that what they call me behind my back? I'm not that tall*, she thought darkly. She despised Whiz O'Neal.

She had to admit, however, that she was curious about Rick because he *was* good-looking and he *had* asked who she was. But then, he had also laughed at her and, she decided, that made him just as much of a creep as Whiz.

Even worse, she would have to be seeing a lot of Rick in the next weeks before Vicki's wedding. *I hate him*, she thought. Still, she couldn't forget what Maria had observed earlier: he sure was cute.

# Chapter Two

After the game, the three girls piled back into Veronica and headed for Emilio's Pizza Palace. Joan seemed to be the only one who was in a good mood as they drove off. She had thoroughly enjoyed the basketball game.

"Peter made some excellent shots tonight," she said to Maria.

"Yeah," Maria agreed absently. Her mind seemed to be somewhere else. She gazed out the car window solemnly.

"Did *you* have a good time?" Joan asked Kim.

"Yeah," Kim replied, staring vacantly at Joan's mop of red curls. Then her eyes moved to Maria's shiny black hair. The three of them made

17

quite a team, she thought. The short brunette, the short redhead and the big, tall blond.

"What's the matter with you two tonight?" Joan asked, breaking the silence.

Her question shook Maria from her daze. "Nothing's wrong," she said, not very convincingly.

"What about you?" Joan asked Kim.

Kim didn't say anything at first. She didn't want to talk about it. Then Maria spoke up. "Kim's upset because of that jerk Whiz O'Neal."

"He *is* pretty gross," Joan agreed.

"I know he's gross, but I was still really embarrassed," Kim said defensively. "And I hate Rick Stone, too," she blurted out suddenly. She quickly regretted having said that because she really had no reason to dislike him so much.

"He does hang out with the wrong crowd," Maria said, digging through her purse. "Do you guys want some gum?" she asked.

Joan shook her head, but Kim took a piece. "Thanks," she said, popping it into her mouth. It seemed to relax her. "What do you know about Rick, anyway?" she asked Maria cautiously.

"Not much. I've never met him," Maria said. "Have you?"

"No," Kim admitted quietly.

"Then why do you hate him?"

Kim scrunched up her nose. "I don't know.

18

He just acts like a creep, I guess." Her voice trailed off weakly.

"Like he did tonight, you mean?" Joan asked.

"It seems as though he's got a big chip on his shoulder," Kim began. "You know how some boys act—as if they're trying to prove to everyone what hotshots they are."

"Oh," Joan replied, not pressing the matter. After a short pause, she asked quietly, "Do you know how his parents died?"

"I don't," Kim said. She had never really thought about it before.

"They were killed in a plane crash," Maria said. "It was in one of those small private planes. They were on their way to some convention. I think it happened about a year ago."

Everyone was very quiet for a moment. "That's awful," Kim said in a tiny voice. She suddenly felt very guilty for thinking such mean thoughts about Rick.

"At first he was put in some boys' boarding school in Oregon. Apparently he hated it there," Maria continued, "so his aunt and uncle, Max's parents, took him in."

"How did you find all this out?" Kim asked. "I see Max all the time, and he never told me any of this stuff."

"My dad worked with Rick's dad on a show once. He was a producer. I can remember when my parents went to the funeral. It was horrible. My mom was upset for days," Maria said in a choked voice. "Right after it happened, my parents seemed to be closer to each other than I'd ever seen them before. It was as if they were really in love." She tried unsuccessfully to muffle a sob. "That's the last time they ever seemed that way to me," she said in a strangled voice.

Kim froze, not sure what to say. Maria's parents had separated a few months earlier, and it looked as though they were going to get a divorce. Kim knew the whole situation upset Maria much more than she let on. "Maria," she asked softly, "how are things going with your parents? Have you heard from your dad?"

Maria regained her control after a loud sniffle. "Yeah. He called my mom yesterday from location," she said. Maria's father was an actor, and he was in Australia filming a TV movie. "He said he's up for the lead in a new series."

"Really? That's great," Kim said, trying to change the mood. She *was* really interested. Maria's father had gotten small parts in several movies for television already, and they all loved to see him when the shows were aired.

"Yeah, his career's really starting to take off," Maria continued with a sigh. "He called my mom yesterday to tell her he wants to go ahead with the divorce. Mom's been crying ever since."

"Oh, Maria," Joan said in a sympathetic voice. "I'm really sorry."

"Yeah, well, I guess there's nothing I can do about it." Maria stared glumly at the dashboard.

"You don't think there's any possibility—" Kim began.

"None," Maria said. "I think he's got a new girlfriend already. At least, that's what my mom thinks."

"I'm sorry," Kim said softly. She wished she could think of something more comforting to say.

"Forget it," Maria said with an effort. "I shouldn't even have brought the whole thing up."

They drove the rest of the way to Emilio's in silence. Just before they got out of the car, Maria turned to them. "I hope I haven't ruined the evening. I shouldn't have dumped all my problems on you guys," she murmured. It looked as though she had regained her self-control. "It's Friday night, after all," she said, forcing a grin. "We should be having fun."

Kim and Joan tried to smile back; they were still troubled by Maria's news.

"Let me just check my makeup," Maria said, flipping down the visor, which had a mirror on the other side. "Veronica!" she exclaimed, sounding as if she were talking to a child. "Your mirror is very dirty." She pulled a tissue out of her purse and quickly wiped it off. "There!" she said. "That's better, isn't it?" Joan and Kim exchanged a glance. Maria was obviously forcing herself to be cheerful.

Emilio's seemed almost as crowded as the gym had been, and they had to wait for an empty table. As they stood in the front, Maria waved and called out to several people she knew, acting very happy and spirited. Kim had to admire her friend's ability to act happy when her life was such a mess. She knew she couldn't handle the situation as well as Maria did.

Once they were seated, they studied the sauce-stained menus the waitress handed them. "What do you guys feel like having?" Joan asked. Her appetite was legendary. But even though she ate and ate, she never gained a pound.

"I don't care," Maria said. "Whatever you guys want."

"You decide," Kim told Joan.

The waitress looked at Joan, waiting for her order. "A large atomic pie," Joan said, naming the house specialty that came with everything on it. "No anchovies, though."

While they waited for their pizza to arrive, Kim studied the crowd. "When's Peter coming?" she asked, turning toward Maria.

Maria looked at her watch. "He should be

here any minute," she said nonchalantly. She didn't even bother to look around for him.

Just after their pizza came, a boy carrying a trash-filled tray stopped at their table. It was Jeff Brubaker, the school's resident computer wizard, and he looked as though he was on his way out. Kim liked him, even though he was a bit of a recluse. He was always busy with his computers.

"How's it going?" Jeff asked them shyly.

"Hi, Jeff," Maria and Kim said in unison. Joan had just taken a big bite of pizza, so she arched an eyebrow at him instead of saying hello.

"Did you guys go to the game?" he asked. Kim noticed that his eyes were glued to Joan.

"Yeah. It was great," Kim said. There was an uncomfortable pause.

"Do you mind if I sit down?" Jeff asked. Before anyone could answer, he plopped himself down in the empty seat next to Joan. Kim was amazed. The Jeff Brubaker she knew was usually too preoccupied with disk drives and microprocessors to sit down and chat. Maria apparently couldn't believe it, either, and she shot Kim a questioning look.

Their surprise grew as Jeff turned his complete attention to Joan. "I hear you got your license," he began. Joan nodded her head and

23

wiped some tomato sauce from her mouth with a napkin. "I'm taking the test in two weeks," Jeff continued. Joan still didn't reply, but she looked as if she were blushing a little.

Jeff paused, and Kim made an effort to fill up the hole in the conversation. "Maybe Joan can give you some pointers," she said brightly, looking at her friend encouragingly. To make sure Joan got the point, Kim gave her a light kick under the table, but Joan didn't bat an eye.

"Maybe we could go over the instruction book together," Jeff suggested doggedly. He was smiling, but he looked as though he were running out of steam.

"OK. If you want to," Joan finally agreed, glaring at Kim. There was no doubt about it anymore. She was turning positively red.

"Great!" Jeff said, getting up quickly. As he stood, he knocked his knee against the table. It seemed as though he could hardly wait to get out of there, and Kim realized that he was just as shy as Joan was. "I'll call you," Jeff said to Joan as he left. Then he took off with his tray.

The minute he was gone Maria turned to Joan. "Really, Joanie," she sputtered. "You're never going to get anywhere with him if you act like that. You have to be warmer, more friendly."

"Who says I want to get anywhere with him?"

Joan demanded, tugging absently at a stray wisp of red hair.

"Well, why not?" Kim broke in. "There's nothing wrong with him. I think he's kind of nice, in fact."

"So do I," Maria agreed.

Joan turned even redder. "You guys—" she began.

"OK, never mind," Maria retorted. "I know it's none of our business." Her voice softened. "We just want you to be happy, Joanie. And even if Jeff's not the boy of your dreams, at least he's a start."

Kim nodded her head in agreement. She was just about to add some more encouraging words when Peter appeared at the table, carrying a huge, overstuffed duffel bag. As soon as he sat down, the girls' conversation stopped. Peter, however, didn't seem to notice.

"Whew," he exhaled with a groan. "I'm beat." He looked at Maria and gave her a broad wink. Maria smiled back.

"Great game, Peter," Joan said immediately, glad that he had arrived. Now she could change the subject to sports—her favorite topic.

"Thanks, Joanie," Peter said, flashing her a big grin. It was no secret that he liked her because she was the only one of Maria's friends he could talk to about basketball.

"That was an incredible shot in the third period," Joan went on.

"Did you like that?" Peter beamed. "I was afraid I was too off-balance to sink it, but I managed to get it in."

"Your rebounding was great tonight, too," Joan added.

Maria rolled her eyes at Kim. Once Joan and Peter started talking about sports, it was hard to get them to stop.

Basking in Joan's compliments, Peter slowly picked up a menu. As he stared at it, Kim idly watched him, lost in thought. Peter was a giant—six foot two—and good-looking in an athletic kind of way. When Maria had started dating him the year before, Kim couldn't help feeling a pang of envy. It was not because he was an all-star athlete, or because he was liked by everyone. She was envious because Peter was so tall. Standing next to someone as tall as Peter made Kim feel petite and feminine. She knew it was a dumb reason to like someone, and a dumb reason to envy Maria, but she couldn't help it.

Her thoughts were interrupted when Peter, Maria, and Joan suddenly broke up laughing over some comment she had missed. Kim wasn't in a mood to laugh, and her eyes moved away from them and swept over the restaurant. As she had at the basketball game, she tried to imagine that somewhere in Emilio's that night sat the boy she would one day love. But somehow she didn't believe it. Sighing, she decided it was just a stupid game.

Peter made another remark, and Joan and Maria laughed even louder. Depressed, Kim dropped her chin on her hands and frowned. Maria had Peter, and even Joan had Jeff interested in her. *When will there be someone for me?* Kim wondered. *When, when, when?*

# Chapter Three

A week later Kim went to the dressmaker's house for the first fitting of her bridesmaid dress.

"I have so much to do. I think I'm going to go crazy," Vicki said to Kim as they drove to the dressmaker's. Vicki drummed her fingers nervously against the steering wheel as if to emphasize her point.

"You've been biting your nails again," Kim said reproachfully, staring at Vicki's hands. "You'd better stop, or they won't grow back in time to look nice at the wedding."

"I know," Vicki said with a guilty expression. "It's such a juvenile habit, but I'm getting so nervous." She glanced at her reflection in the

28

rearview mirror and sighed. "And I have to do something about my hair. It's so blah. Should I get it permed again?"

Kim studied Vicki's sandy-blond hair. It was just a little darker than her own, but much shorter. "If you decide to, you'd better do it at least a week before the wedding so it won't look too frizzy."

"You're right," she said distractedly. "Where's my appointment book?" she asked, glancing around the front seat.

"I'll find it. You drive," Kim said. The front seat of the car looked like a disaster area. Among the articles strewn around the two seats were fabric swatches, a book of sample thank-you cards, a floor plan of the Palms Hotel ballroom. Numerous lists of things to do had been scribbled on scraps of paper and taped to the dashboard. Vicki was famous for her disorganization. She could even be slightly ditsy at times, but she always managed to pull things together when she had to.

"I found it," Kim said triumphantly, pulling the appointment book out from under a pair of sneakers on the floor in front of her. "When do you want to schedule it?" she asked. She found a pen sticking out of the tissue box on the dashboard.

"Two weeks before the wedding," Vicki said "That should be enough time, don't you think?"

Kim grunted her agreement and wrote, "Perm hair" in for Saturday, January 31. Then she closed the book and carefully placed it next to her on the seat. She began to stack everything up neatly. Unlike her sister, Kim was always very organized.

"Did I bring the fabric swatch?" Vicki murmured, almost as if she were talking to herself.

"Vicki," Kim said in a stern voice, "you have to calm down. Everything is going to be fine."

Vicki shot her a weary glance. "That's easy for you to say," she replied, staring pointedly at Kim. "I've got a trillion things to do in just four weeks."

"Maybe you should have given yourselves more time," Kim observed. "Since you're taking the whole semester off, you could have waited until April to get married."

Vicki sighed. "I know. But we wanted to get married on Valentine's Day. It seems so romantic. And that will give us enough time to find a house and get settled in Vermont before we start the summer term. Anyway," she continued, "it's done. If I can just make it through the wedding, everything will be fine."

"I'll help if you want," Kim said. Even though she had offered her assistance several times,

Vicki had turned her down. She seemed determined to do everything herself.

"Thanks, but there's really nothing I need you to do." Vicki knit her brow. "Wait. There *is* something," she said. "Can you find the swatch for the tablecloths?"

"It's here somewhere," Kim said, fumbling through the piles. Finally she pulled a pink square of fabric from between the pages of the guest list for the reception.

"All right," Vicki said in a serious tone, "this is what you have to do." She cleared her throat as though she were going to say something of earth-shaking importance. "Make sure the bridesmaids' outfits match the color of this swatch," she said slowly. "Exactly. Understand?"

Kim nodded her head and suppressed a groan. Sometimes Vicki treated her as though she were a baby. "I think I can handle it," she replied dryly. She couldn't understand why the tablecloths and the bridesmaids' dresses had to be the same color, anyway. Somehow the idea of blending in with the furniture didn't thrill her.

"If they don't match exactly," Vicki continued, "call me. I'll be at the printer's. I think the number is on the back of that sales slip," she said, pointing to a piece of paper taped to the glove compartment.

Kim wrote down the number dutifully. She

knew there was no point in trying to argue with Vicki about it. These days Vicki scarcely listened to a word anyone said. Her mind was going in a thousand directions at once, and Kim couldn't help feeling a little resentful. They used to be so close, but now that Vicki was getting married, Kim could feel that closeness slipping away.

They pulled up to the dressmaker's house. It was a tiny stucco bungalow nestled in a bunch of palm trees. "Say hi to everybody for me," Vicki said as she eased the car to a stop. Kim nodded her head and got out. "And don't forget to call me if the color's not exactly the same," Vicki added, leaning out the window. "I'll pick you up on my way back." With that, she drove away.

Kim reluctantly walked up the path to the house. Although she had managed to forget about it while she was with Vicki, she was dreading the fitting. Kim was convinced that the dress would make her look like a giant. A pang of anxiety ran through her when she got to the door.

The other two bridesmaids, Spring and Elaine, were already there.

"Boy, you've really grown since the last time I saw you," Elaine said to Kim the moment she saw her. It wasn't exactly what Kim had wanted to hear, but she tried to smile politely. Spring gave her a kiss. Then Max's little sister, Anne, came tearing around a corner, holding a large cookie. Kim bent down and gave the child a hug. Anne was six years old and she was going to be the flower girl.

Mrs. Garcia, the dressmaker, emerged from the fitting room. Her salt-and-pepper hair needed combing, and she had a pincushion strapped to her wrist that looked like some kind of futuristic watch. Over her other arm she carried one of the dresses she was making. She set it down on the sewing table beside Kim.

Just then, Elaine diverted Mrs. Garcia's attention with a question, and Kim slid the tablecloth swatch from her pocket and put it next to the dress to compare the colors. They were a perfect match, and she breathed a sigh of relief. At least she wouldn't have to call Vicki with something else to worry her.

"All right, girls," Mrs. Garcia said in a heavy Spanish accent. "Who wants to go first?" When nobody answered, Mrs. Garcia took little Anne by the hand and led her into the fitting room.

"I hope they look good," Spring said nervously to Elaine. Kim was relieved to find out that she wasn't the only one who was concerned.

"Don't worry. The dresses will be fine," Elaine

replied with the weary air of someone who had been a bridesmaid several times before.

Five minutes later Anne came out, and Spring and Elaine gasped with delight at how cute she looked. The dress, made of pink taffeta, had a dropped waist and a lace collar. It looked so appealing on Anne that Kim's spirits rose temporarily. Then she realized that Anne was wearing the pint-size version.

Mrs. Garcia beckoned to Kim and then led her into the fitting room. As Kim removed her sweater and jeans, she was reminded of the first time she had visited the dressmaker. She'd gone to have her measurements taken. Even though Mrs. Garcia hadn't said anything, Kim was sure she had thought she had a giant on her hands. Her fears were reinforced when Mrs. Garcia kept asking Kim to stand up straight.

Mrs. Garcia slipped the dress over Kim's head. "Hmmm," she murmured as she stepped back to look Kim over.

Kim nervously moved to stand in front of the dressing-room mirror and surveyed her pink reflection. Her heart sank. The dress didn't flatter her at all, just as she had suspected. If anything, she looked like an overgrown child. Or a giant pink Popsicle. She felt so bad she wanted to cry, but she restrained herself. She didn't want to hurt Mrs. Garcia's feelings.

"It needs some fixing," Mrs. Garcia said calmly, pulling a bunch of pins from the cushion on her arm. Then she began taking tucks in the bodice. *Why bother*, Kim thought dejectedly. *Nothing can make this dress look good on me.*

When Mrs. Garcia had finished, she led Kim out to the living room to model it for the others. This time, though, Spring and Elaine didn't gasp in delight.

"How sweet," Spring finally said.

"Yes, it's very—sweet," Elaine agreed, but her face gave her away. Elaine obviously knew what she was in for.

Kim's suspicions proved to be correct. Elaine's dress made her look as though she were wearing oversize doll clothes. And Spring didn't fare much better. The mood in the living room changed considerably.

Mrs. Garcia must have sensed the girls' disappointment because when the fitting was over, she assured them all that the dresses would look much better after the alterations had been made. On that hopeful note, Spring and Elaine got up to go. Just before they left, Elaine turned to Kim.

"Oh. I forgot to tell you, Kim," she said with a smile. "We're going to throw a surprise shower for Vicki at the Marina. It's going to be Thursday the twenty-second, and we really want you to come."

"Sure," Kim said, flushing slightly. She was kind of flattered to be invited to a college-age gathering.

"Bring two gifts—a serious one and a gag gift," Spring said. "You know, something funny. Or something cute." With a wave of her hand, she followed Elaine out the door.

Kim smiled. In her mind, she went through her closet, trying to decide what she should wear to the shower. When she couldn't think of anything, she turned her thoughts to what she could buy for the gifts. Again she drew a blank.

Mrs. Garcia came out of the kitchen and offered her a glass of iced tea from the pitcher she had brought with her. Kim nodded, and Mrs. Garcia poured her a glass. She gave Anne some chocolate milk. Kim glanced at her watch. Vicki was fifteen minutes late, which was not all that surprising. Whoever was picking Anne up was late, too, but the little girl didn't seem to care. She was too busy examining the beautiful clothing on a little doll that Mrs. Garcia had given her to play with.

Then Kim heard a car drive up and a door slam. *It's Vicki at last*, she thought. Kim gave Anne a quick kiss, then tugged on the front door, which seemed to be stuck. It opened after a hard yank, and Kim turned her head and called goodbye to Mrs. Garcia.

She wasn't paying attention to where she was going and crashed into the person who was coming in. They collided for an instant, then both drew back just as quickly and looked at each other in astonishment. Kim wanted to die. It was Rick.

Rick looked at her strangely, then chuckled good-naturedly.

Kim, feeling like the clumsiest person alive, glared at him. Under any other circumstances, she probably would have thought the situation was funny, too. It was her fault, after all—she hadn't been looking. But Rick's laughter reminded her of the last time she had seen him. He had been laughing then, too, because Whiz O'Neal had called her Kim Kong.

"Excuse me," Kim managed to say in a cold voice. "I thought you were my sister."

"Do you usually run into her?" Rick asked, arching his eyebrows.

Even though he was being friendly, Kim was convinced that he was mocking her. "No, I don't," she replied. With as much dignity as she could muster, she spun around and went back into the living room. She plunked herself down on the couch angrily, her heart racing.

"Well, *excuse* me," she heard Rick mutter. Out of the corner of her eye, she saw him enter the room. "Hi," he said to Mrs. Garcia. "Come on, Annie," he said to the little girl.

Anne ran over to Rick, and he scooped her up and swung her in the air. She giggled with delight. Rick whirled her around again and said, "Annie, Annie, Annie" very fast. Anne giggled even harder. It was obvious to Kim that Anne adored him.

Then Rick let Anne climb up on his back and he gave her a piggyback ride to the front door. "So long," he said to Mrs. Garcia. He set Anne down gently and turned to look at Kim. "Nice bumping into you," he said to her with a wry grin before disappearing out the door.

Kim scowled. *What a rude comment,* she thought darkly. But somehow, she couldn't get all that mad about it. He hadn't ignored her totally as he had the first time they had met at school. He'd even spoken to her this time and tried to joke with her. He was very attractive, too. And *very* tall. Kim felt confused.

"He's the little girl's cousin," Mrs. Garcia said to Kim, startling her. Kim had almost forgotten where she was. "Such a nice boy," Mrs. Garcia added with a conspiratorial smile.

Kim managed to nod her head, and she flashed Mrs. Garcia an uneasy grin. She was getting embarrassed. The dressmaker was trying to fix her up with Rick Stone! Kim heard another car pull up out front. This time she looked out the window first and saw that it was Vicki.

"Thanks for the iced tea," Kim said politely to Mrs. Garcia. She yanked on the front door. Instead of sticking, it flew open easily. *Just my luck*, she thought.

Vicki barely looked up when Kim slid into the seat beside her. "How did it go?" she asked distractedly, running her finger down a long list. Before Kim had a chance to answer, Vicki continued, "Did the swatch match the dresses?"

"Yes," Kim said.

"Exactly?"

"Yes, exactly," Kim said. "What are you looking at?"

"The guest list for the reception," Vicki said slowly. Turning to look at Kim, she asked, "Should I ask Bonnie Stokes?"

"Who's Bonnie Stokes?" Kim asked, not really caring. She couldn't believe Vicki hadn't asked how the dresses looked.

"Bonnie was my best friend in third grade," Vicki said, looking at her list again. In the next breath she asked, "How do the dresses look?" Her mind was obviously going in a thousand directions at once.

Kim swallowed hard. "Nice," she said brightly, trying to work up some enthusiasm. She thought for a moment. "Anne looks just adorable in hers," she continued truthfully.

"Oh, good," Vicki murmured. "Did Max come to pick her up?" Her voice almost cracked when she said his name. Vicki was definitely in love.

"No," Kim said, clearing her throat. "Rick did." She tried to make her voice sound light.

"He's cute, isn't he?" Vicki remarked with a mischievous smile.

Kim shrugged noncommittally. "He's OK," she said.

"That's all you have to say? Just 'He's OK'?" Vicki's dimples flashed, and her gaze darted over to Kim. "I especially wanted him in the wedding party for your sake. If I were your age, I'd think he was pretty neat."

Kim couldn't believe it. First the dressmaker and now her own sister was trying to fix her up with Rick Stone. "He's OK," Kim insisted stubbornly. Vicki took the hint and dropped the subject.

# Chapter Four

On Monday afternoon the temperature soared to eighty degrees. Kim was at band practice, and she wiped a bead of perspiration from her eyebrow as she scanned the other band members, looking for Joan.

Then, at the far end of the football field, she saw someone emerge from the girls' locker room. The figure trotted briskly across the field, and even that far away, Kim could see the red hair and knew that it was Joan. Kim waved her clarinet in the air to attract Joan's attention.

"Where have you been?" Kim demanded when Joan got there.

"I lost the key to my locker," Joan said sheepishly. "Wouldn't you know it would be this hot

41

the one day we have formation practice?" she added.

Kim nodded her head in disgust, roasting in her white blazer and pants. The band was going to march in the Easter parade downtown, so they had been practicing more than ever lately. They had only six weeks to choreograph the whole thing. Kim stretched, throwing her head back. The cloudless sky looked almost white instead of blue. *How can it be so hot in January?* she wondered.

"Why is everyone standing around?" Joan asked.

"Mr. Banfield wants to rechoreograph the last formation," Kim replied, studying Joan's face. Somehow she looked different that day. Her cheeks had a lot of color, for one thing, but Kim decided that they were flushed from Joan's sprint across the field.

"What was wrong with the formation?"

"It was a disaster." Kim giggled at the thought of it. "Everybody kept bumping into one another, and Paul Huntley collided with somebody and scratched the tuba. Mr. Banfield had an absolute conniption."

Joan turned her head to look at their band instructor, and when she did, Kim got a good look at her profile. To her amazement, she realized Joan's cheeks weren't flushed at all. Joan was wearing blusher.

"What's that?" Kim asked, pointing to Joan's cheek.

"Really!" Joan exclaimed, glaring at her. "It's no big deal. Just a little makeup." She tried to make it sound as though she wore makeup every day.

"Since when—" Kim began. Then she stopped and looked at Joan more closely. "You're wearing mascara, too!"

"So? You and Maria are always trying to talk me into putting some on."

"Don't get me wrong, I like it," Kim said immediately. "It looks good, it really does. You have to blend the blusher in a little more here, though." With her fingertips, she smoothed the blusher more evenly over Joan's left cheekbone. "There," Kim said. "Perfect."

"Thanks." Joan relaxed, and a timid expression came over her face. "There's something I want to ask you."

"Anything," Kim replied.

"Do you know anything about hair straighteners?"

"Hair straighteners?"

"Yes. I don't want my hair to be straight, just not so curly."

Kim examined Joan's curly red mop. "It looks cute that way," she protested. Then Kim stopped. Something was up, she was sure of it. "Wait a minute," she said. "What's going on here? Why are you going through this big transformation all of a sudden?" She narrowed her eyes and looked at Joan intensely. "What's happened?"

"It's not such a big transformation," Joan protested weakly. Kim shot her a look of disbelief. "Well," Joan confessed, moving a step closer to Kim so she could whisper into her ear, "Jeff called me up and asked me out."

"That's fantastic!" Kim replied. "Finally. To help him study for his driver's test?"

"No, he didn't even mention the test," Joan said shyly. "He asked me to go to the movies. Should I have said no?"

"What do you mean?" Kim asked, a bit perplexed. "Don't you like Jeff?"

"Sure I do," Joan assured her friend. "I meant that I said I'd go out with him when he called. Should I have said I was busy and then waited for him to ask me out again?"

"Are you kidding? If you like somebody, you have to be honest with him and not play games." Kim shook her clarinet at Joan to emphasize her point. "You want to go, right?"

"Kind of, yeah," Joan said, lowering her eyes, embarrassed.

"Then you did the right thing," Kim said emphatically. Joan was making her feel as though she were the world's authority on dating. "When's your date?"

"Friday. Do you think I could get my hair straightened by then? I don't have the slightest idea where to go. Do you think it's expensive?" Joan was full of questions.

"I think you should wait for a while before you do anything that drastic," Kim suggested. "You might change your mind. Besides, you want Jeff to recognize you, don't you?" she added with a sly grin.

Joan thought it over. "I guess you're right. We have to talk about it more, though." Just then, Mr. Banfield blew two short blasts on his whistle to signal the band to get into starting position.

"OK," Kim agreed. "Call me later." Joan smiled and they took their positions.

When Kim got home from band practice, she felt a little depressed. Even though she was happy that Joan had a date, it made her feel even more left out than ever. If both Maria and Joan had steady boyfriends, would they still have time for her? she wondered. Admittedly, Joan was only going out on a first date, but what if she and Jeff became a steady couple?

The house was quiet, and Kim looked around to see if anyone was home. She realized her mother must be home because a roast was cooking in the oven, and the kitchen table was covered with menus. Kim's mother had taken charge of the luncheon at the wedding reception.

Walking into the hallway, Kim saw her mother's shoes placed neatly in the corner. She must have just gotten home from work, Kim thought.

Kim's hunch was correct. She found her mother in the dining room, still wearing the beige suit she had been wearing when she left for work that morning. "Hi, Mom," Kim called.

"Hi, honey." Mrs. Sommers looked slightly frazzled as she hurriedly set the table. "How's my baby?"

"Fine," Kim said, giving her a hug. "Who's not going to be here for dinner tonight?" she asked, noticing that there were only three places set on the table.

"Your sister," Mrs. Sommers replied. "She's having dinner at Max's."

"Oh." Once Vicki moved away, Kim thought sadly, there would always be only three places set at the table. The thought upset her more than she cared to admit.

"Sweetheart," Kim's mother said, studying her daughter's downcast expression, "what's wrong? You don't look very happy."

Kim hung her head. How could she possibly explain how she was feeling to her mom? It seemed so selfish.

"Now stand up straight," her mother continued. Kim's bad posture was one of her mother's pet peeves. Kim obeyed meekly. "Look at me," Mrs. Sommers said. "Now, tell me what's the matter."

Kim took a deep breath. All of her problems were ready to tumble out. But just then the phone rang.

"That's probably the caterer. I'm expecting a call," her mother explained. "You wait right here because I want to talk to you. This will only take a minute." Her mother disappeared into the kitchen.

Kim slumped dejectedly into a dining room chair, resting her chin in her hands. She could hear her mother on the phone in the kitchen, and the conversation seemed to be taking forever. After a while her mother wandered back into the dining room, the phone cradled on her neck, pulling the extra long phone cord after her.

"Mr. Shypert," Mrs. Sommers was saying to

the caterer, "I thought we agreed that crabmeat was too expensive for my budget." She picked up a handful of utensils and continued setting the table as she spoke. She seemed to have forgotten all about Kim.

With a sigh, Kim stood up and helped her mother. Maybe her problems weren't so important, she decided. Her mom did have a lot on her mind. Still, she couldn't help feeling sorry for herself.

"Yes, rack of lamb is fine for the entrée," her mother continued. She motioned for Kim to get water glasses out of the sideboard in the dining room. "I prefer lamb to prime rib," she said into the phone. Then she began a long discussion about the choice of vegetables.

Kim helped finish setting the table in a daze. When she was done, she stood in front of her mother awkwardly. "I'm going up to my room until dinner," she mumbled.

Her mother cupped her hand over the mouthpiece. "What?" she said in a whisper.

"I'll be in my room," Kim repeated.

"Oh, OK." Her mother nodded distractedly and waved her hand. The caterer had evidently been speaking to her the whole time. "I see," she said into the phone.

Kim backed out of the dining room. She knew

she shouldn't feel hurt, but her mother's gesture almost made her feel that she was being dismissed.

Completely frustrated, Kim went upstairs to her room. Passing Vicki's door, she heard her sister moving around so she stopped and knocked. "Vicki?" she called tentatively. Maybe her sister had time to talk.

"It's open," Vicki replied.

Vicki was in the middle of getting dressed, and Kim thought she looked especially pretty. She was wearing one of her best outfits, a plum-colored silk dress that Kim had always admired.

"How do I look?" Vicki asked, swiveling in front of her mirror. "I haven't worn this dress since last year. Is it too tight in the back?"

Kim could tell from the look in Vicki's eyes that she didn't have time to talk, either. "It looks fine," she replied, suppressing a sigh. "Mom said you're going to Max's tonight."

"Uh-huh," Vicki said, holding a purse against her dress to see if they looked good together. "It's Max's parents' wedding anniversary," she explained. She moved over to her closet and surveyed the shoe boxes stacked on the shelves. "What time is it?" she asked. She pulled out a box from the bottom of the stack, and suddenly the entire pile of shoe boxes came tumbling to the floor. "Honestly!" Vicki exclaimed in exasperation.

Kim glanced at her watch. "It's six-thirty."

"Oh, no, I'm going to be late," Vicki moaned, triumphantly pulling out the shoes she was searching for from a box that had fallen open on the floor. She put the shoes on, slipped her bag under her arm, and struck a pose. "Does this look dressy enough?" she asked Kim.

"Very chic," Kim answered truthfully.

"Good." Vicki began transferring the contents of her everyday purse into the dressier one. "Listen," she added, "could you do me a gigantic favor?"

"What?"

"Could you put the shoes that fell out back in their boxes?" Vicki asked with a pleading look on her face. "Mom'll have a fit if she sees this mess, and I just don't have time to clean it up." Kim knew her sister was right. Her mother always nagged Vicki about her sloppiness, just as she nagged Kim about her posture.

"OK," Kim muttered in a defeated tone.

Vicki paused at the door, hearing the hurt in Kim's voice. "You don't have to arrange them on the shelf," she said in a conciliatory tone. "Just stack them inside the closet on the floor."

"No problem."

Vicki continued to stare at her sister as if she

knew something was wrong. She made one last effort to cheer Kim up. "I'll say hi to Rick for you tonight, kiddo," she said with a grin.

"Don't bother," Kim said frostily, walking over to the closet. She bent over and began sorting through the pile of shoes.

Vicki looked anxiously at her watch. "I don't know what's upsetting you, Kimmie," she said, trying to be sympathetic, "but I'm late. I'll have time to talk about it later, though. We can gab for as long as you want when I get home, OK?"

"OK," Kim said, softening. At least her sister understood that something was wrong. "Do me one favor," she said to Vicki, feeling bolder. "Don't say anything to Rick about me. I'll tell you why later."

Vicki looked puzzled, but she didn't ask any questions. "Whatever you say," she said, and after giving herself a squirt of perfume, she left.

Kim straightened up Vicki's shoes, then went into her room and threw herself on her bed. She had a terrible urge to play her Madonna album at full volume, but she knew it drove her mother crazy, so she just lay there, staring at a chip in the paint on the ceiling above her bed.

Why did everyone think that she liked Rick, she wondered. He was just an arrogant snob who made a lot of rude jokes all the time. But even as she told herself how terrible he was,

51

she couldn't get the image of his warm brown eyes out of her mind. When they had bumped into each other at Mrs. Garcia's, his eyes were the first thing she saw, and they had burned themselves into her memory.

"I *hate* him," she mumbled out loud, trying to sound convinced. If only she could get herself to believe it.

# Chapter Five

After class on Thursday Kim met Maria in the school parking lot. They had arranged several days before to go shopping with Peter for a new stereo for his car. When Kim arrived, Maria seemed upset. She tossed her head and impatiently drummed her fingernails on the top of Peter's red MG.

"Where's Peter?" Kim asked carefully. Maria looked as though she was in a dangerous mood.

"Late, as usual," Maria retorted. "He makes me so mad sometimes." She ran her fingers through her black hair and frowned.

"What happened?"

"Well, I've been a little—uh—upset lately," Maria began. Kim nodded sympathetically. "Oh,

Kim, he doesn't even care. He just tells me to quit moping around," Maria said hotly, her eyes flashing. "He's so insensitive sometimes. Just a big dumb jock. All he wants to do is party all the time."

"Is everything OK at home?" Kim asked quietly. Her parents, Kim thought, were the real reason Maria was so upset.

Maria lowered her eyes. "As good as can be expected, I guess. My mom is handling the whole thing a little better. I guess she's getting used to the idea of the divorce."

Kim didn't know what to say. She was almost sorry she'd brought the whole thing up.

Maria obviously didn't want to discuss it, either. "What am I going to do about Peter?" she asked.

Even though Peter was kind of a dumb jock, Kim still liked him. She knew deep down that he was a nice person and good for Maria. "He probably doesn't understand what you're going through," Kim said. "I think he just wants you to be happy, and he's trying to help the only way he knows how. There's nothing you can do about the situation at home except to try to give your mother as much love and support as you can."

Kim was surprised to hear Maria admit that she didn't have everything under control. Maria seemed to have everything: looks, brains, poise, popularity. But even Maria had problems. Kim's own difficulties suddenly didn't seem so unique.

Maria made an effort to brighten up. She changed the subject. "Joanie called me on Monday night," she began, a faint smile playing on her lips.

"Isn't it great?" Kim said enthusiastically. They both had been hoping for a long time that Joan would find a boyfriend. "I'm so excited for her."

Maria warmed to the subject, prodded by Kim's enthusiasm. "She asked me a million questions."

"Me, too," Kim said. "She wants a totally new look for her date tomorrow night."

"She asked me about curl relaxers! Can you believe it? Our Joanie?" Maria exclaimed. "One day you couldn't even talk her into using lip gloss, and the next day she wants her hair straightened."

"It was all an act before," Kim said confidentially. "She was so shy around boys that she just pretended she didn't care about them. But she really did."

Maria agreed. "I hope it works out all right— for her sake," she said, crossing her fingers. "If it doesn't, we'll never be able to talk her into wearing makeup again," she said with another grin. "Or going on another date."

But Maria's smile faded as soon as she spotted Peter coming toward them across the parking lot. Her mood changed instantly as though a curtain had been drawn over her. Kim was disappointed. She had hoped she would be able to shake Maria out of her gloomy thoughts.

"Hi," Peter said casually as he drew up to the car. He was wearing the loudest Hawaiian shirt Kim had ever seen. He glanced at Maria as if to study her face for a clue to her mood. Maria moved away from his car and stared off into the distance, refusing to look him in the eye. Peter decided to ignore her.

He unlocked the car and fumbled under the dashboard for the button that released the top of the convertible. "Give me a hand, would you?" he asked.

Maria remained rooted firmly to the spot where she stood, so Kim stepped over and helped Peter pull the top down. It was a wonderfully warm, sunny day, and she was looking forward to riding in the open car, with the wind blowing through her hair.

After Peter helped Kim crawl into the tiny backseat, he turned to Maria. "Are you coming or not, Miss Mopey?" he asked, trying to make it sound like a joke. But he barely disguised the irritation in his voice.

Without replying, Maria flounced over to the car, got in, and slammed the door shut. In the backseat, Kim rolled her eyes. Despite the glorious weather, she could see it wasn't going to be a pleasant trip.

The stereo store was about a half hour away, and Peter took the road along the ocean. Kim ignored the obvious tension between Peter and Maria and concentrated on the beauty of the day and the tangy smell of the sea air.

There was no conversation at all in the front seat. Peter yelled something back at Kim every now and then, but the wind whipping around them made it impossible to have a real conversation, and he finally gave up. Maria sat in stony silence, oblivious of everything around her.

When they reached Peabody's Stereo Heaven, Kim tried to act as if everything were normal. "What kind of car stereo are you going to get?" she asked Peter, making conversation.

"I'm thinking about getting a CD player," Peter replied. "If I can afford it. I'm afraid I've only saved enough for a cassette player, though." He got out of the car and went around to open the door for Maria. She ignored his thoughtful gesture, and the irritated look was still on her face.

Inside Peabody's, an instrumental version of "The Look of Love" played on the intercom. *Perfect choice*, Kim thought. Peter wandered over to inspect a display of high-power speakers, leaving the two girls standing alone. "What's he doing?" Maria hissed. "I haven't got all day!"

"Please stop this," Kim said under her breath. The last thing she wanted to witness was a big fight in public.

"Where are the CD players, anyway?" Maria demanded, her eyes scanning the immense store. "Aren't there any salespeople in here?" she continued. Then she spotted a tall boy stacking boxes behind a counter.

Maria strode over to the clerk. His back was to them, but Maria didn't wait for him to turn around before she spoke. "We're looking for CD players," she announced. Her tone made it clear that she was in no mood to fool around.

Something about the clerk's back looked familiar to Kim, and an uneasy feeling came over her. The clerk turned around, and she saw it was Rick.

"CD players are in aisle six," he said automatically. "If you'd like to see anything in particular, just ask." Then a look of recognition came over his face as he realized to whom he was talking. He almost looked as though he were about to smile.

Maria didn't bat an eye, though. Much to Kim's embarrassment, she didn't even acknowledge his presence. "And where is aisle six?" Maria demanded coldly.

"Over there." Rick pointed across the store, flushing at her brusqueness.

"That says aisle five," Maria replied, pointing to a sign hanging from the ceiling.

"Sorry," Rick mumbled. "I got mixed up. That's the aisle I meant."

"Well, make up your mind," Maria said in a haughty voice. "Which aisle *is* it?"

"Aisle five." Rick stared at the floor in embarrassment.

Maria took off without another word. Kim remained frozen in front of the counter. She felt sorry for Rick, and at the same time she felt guilty about her own rudeness to him the last time she had seen him—at Mrs. Garcia's.

"Hello," Kim stammered. The word seemed to pop out of her mouth automatically, and she immediately felt silly. Rick looked at her, still a little flushed. "We seem to be running into each other a lot lately," she said nervously, trying to act casual. There was a long, uncomfortable pause. She took a deep breath. "We've never been formally introduced," she said, surprised at her own boldness. "I'm Kim Sommers."

"I know who you are," Rick said. He seemed on the verge of exploding. "What I don't understand is why you hang around with that snob," he said, nodding his head in Maria's direction.

"She's not a snob," Kim replied angrily. Although she *did* seem that way that day, Kim added to herself.

"She thinks *she's* a movie star just because her dad was on a couple of TV shows," Rick said, his brown eyes stone cold. His gaze fell on Peter. "She only goes out with him because he's the captain of the basketball team."

Kim was surprised that he knew so much about them. He always seemed so detached. Still, Maria was her friend. "That's not really fair," she shot back angrily. "Maria's not a snob at all."

"It's the truth," Rick said stubbornly. His face seemed to be getting redder and redder.

"You're not much better," Kim retorted. "You're hardly one to talk about being a snob." It was the only thing she could think to say, but as soon as the words were out of her mouth, she regretted it. Rick looked stunned, as though he had been slapped. Spinning on his heel, he turned and resumed stacking the boxes behind the counter. But even though his back was to her, she could see that his hands were shaking.

Kim awkwardly shifted her feet. She had only been trying to be pleasant, to strike up a conversation. They were going to be seeing a lot of each other over the next few weeks, and she had wanted to be friendly. But she'd only been wasting her time trying to be nice, she decided.

Rick was as stuck-up and rude as she had thought he would be.

Without another word, Kim left the store and went out to the parking lot. She didn't want to be with Peter and Maria; she needed to be alone. There was too much on her mind.

Climbing into the backseat of Peter's car, Kim folded her arms tightly against her, fuming. What a fool she'd been! Rick Stone wasn't worth talking to, let alone trying to be friends with.

Her anger over the incident at Peabody's was put aside that evening, the night of Vicki's surprise shower. She was so concerned about what to wear that she didn't have time to think about Rick. She hoped the outfit she had selected—an oversize blue pullover and her new pink skirt—looked good enough for Vicki's college friends.

As they had planned, Kim told Vicki that she and her mother were going to the mall. But instead of going there, they drove to the Marina.

"What did you get your sister for a present?" her mother asked, looking at the two gifts Kim held in her lap. Her mother had been so busy that Kim hadn't even bothered to consult her when she had gone shopping.

"Well," Kim said, "for the joke gift I got a squirting engagement ring."

"A what?"

"A trick ring, you know. The kind that squirts water," Kim explained, hoping it didn't sound too juvenile.

"Oh," Mrs. Sommers said, looking doubtfully at her daughter. "Where did you get it?"

"The boardwalk. And for her real gift, I got her a copper teakettle," Kim quickly added.

"That sounds nice," her mother said. "Did your father give you some money for them?"

Kim wrinkled her nose. "The gifts are from *me*, Mom. I want to pay for them myself, out of my allowance."

Her mother smiled proudly. "Well, if you need some extra money this week—" she began.

"Don't worry, Mom," Kim said. "I can handle it." *It was sweet of her to offer, though,* Kim thought.

Her mom dropped Kim off at the Marina, with the understanding that she would come home with Vicki. After the car drove away, Kim felt a few butterflies in her stomach. She didn't know anyone who was going to be at the party except for Elaine and Spring, and she didn't even know them very well. Swallowing hard, she pushed her way through the heavy oak doors of the Marina.

The Marina was decorated in a nautical motif, and the hostess directed her past the fish-ing nets strung on a wall to the private room where the party was being held. When she opened the door, a hush fell over the room and everyone turned to see who it was.

"Oh, it's you, Kim," Spring exclaimed. "I thought it might be the guest of honor. This is Kim, everybody," she said to the others. "Vicki's little sister."

Kim smiled bashfully. She liked being introduced as "little" for a change. The other girls smiled back and said hello. Then Spring led her over to a box covered with crepe paper. "This is the wishing well. It's for your joke present." Kim dutifully deposited the squirting engagement ring in the box, hoping it wasn't too stupid. "How about some punch?" Spring asked.

Kim nodded. She was impressed at all the work they had done to organize the shower. Besides the punch, there was a large buffet of cold cuts and a heart-shaped cake. On the wall was a big blown-up photograph of Vicki and Max holding hands.

Kim was just about to take a sip of punch when Elaine entered, dragging Vicki behind her. "I think this is the way upstairs," Elaine was saying, trying hard not to laugh.

Vicki stopped dead in her tracks in the doorway. Everyone yelled "Surprise!"

Vicki's eyes popped in disbelief. "You guys

. . ." she gasped. Her whole face lit up in a huge grin.

The evening turned out far better than Kim had imagined it would. The other girls were very friendly, and several of them told Vicki what a cute sister she had. They made Kim feel so welcome that soon she completely forgot her nervousness.

Vicki opened the gag gifts in the wishing well, and Kim was relieved that her gift wasn't as dumb as she'd feared. Some of the other gifts—a T-shirt that said "I'M WITH STUPID" and a copy of the *I Hate To Cook Cookbook* that had nothing but blank pages—were even dumber, she decided. But Vicki seemed to think all of them were wonderful. She opened each gift amid screams of laughter. Kim was glad to see Vicki relaxed and enjoying herself instead of running around worrying about everything she had to do.

After Vicki had unwrapped all the gag presents, she opened the real gifts. She seemed particularly thrilled with Kim's copper teakettle and gave her sister a big hug. "I'm so happy you're going to be one of my bridesmaids," she whispered in her ear. Kim beamed.

After all the gifts had been opened, Spring and Elaine took the bows from each package and taped them to a paper plate, making a hat for Vicki. She posed for pictures in it, making crazy faces.

The evening seemed to speed by, and before Kim knew it, she and Vicki were driving home. "How long have you known about this?" Vicki asked with a twinkle in her eye.

"Since last week."

"You're pretty good at keeping secrets, aren't you?" Vicki said, smiling.

Kim smiled, too. For some reason, a vision of Rick's face suddenly flashed through her mind.

Vicki must have read her mind. "I have to apologize," she said quietly, "for teasing you about Rick. I promise not to do it anymore."

"I don't really care," Kim murmured. But she noticed that her heart had started to pound at the mention of his name.

# Chapter Six

On a hazy Saturday afternoon two days later Kim shuffled down the street to catch the bus to Mrs. Garcia's for the second fitting of her bridesmaid's dress. She wasn't in a very happy mood. On top of her doubts about the dress, her mother had dropped a bombshell just before she left. On the Sunday before the wedding, Max's family would be giving a dinner for both of their families, and obviously Kim had to attend. To Kim, the dinner meant only one thing: another meeting with Rick Stone. Even though it was two weeks away, she dreaded it.

When she got to the bus stop, she looked around impatiently. Kim hated taking the bus, but she had no choice. She had arranged for

Joan to drive her to Mrs. Garcia's, but Joan had called earlier that day to say that Veronica had broken down and was in the repair shop. Since nobody at home had time to take her, that left only the bus for transportation. To Kim's surprise, Joan had insisted on going with her anyway.

Joan had given her a signal phone call just before she left so they'd catch the same bus. When it finally pulled into view, Kim saw Joan's red hair and a freckled hand, waving out of one of the windows.

"Hi," Kim said after she'd made her way to the middle of the bus where Joan was sitting. She noticed Joan was wearing a pair of culottes, instead of her usual jeans. "Cute outfit," Kim said.

"Thanks," Joan replied. She had on a little more makeup than she was wearing the last time Kim had seen her. Joan had done something different with her hair, too. Although it was as curly as ever, she had pulled the left side back and fastened it with a large tortoiseshell barrette. It seemed to open her face up and dramatize her high cheekbones.

"You look fantastic," Kim said as she looked Joan up and down. She brushed off the green plastic seat next to Joan and sat down.

Joan grinned at her compliment. "Do you like my hair this way?" she asked anxiously.

"It looks super," Kim assured her. "I'm glad you left it curly, though." It seemed funny to Kim to be talking about hairstyles with Joan.

"Good," Joan replied, almost as though she were talking to herself. She leaned over to Kim confidentially, then paused as if searching for the right words.

Kim could tell from the look in her eyes that something was up. "What?" she demanded.

"I had my date with Jeff last night." Joan's blue eyes almost sparkled when she said it.

"And?" Kim prompted her, feeling a little ashamed. She had been so concerned with herself that she had completely forgotten about Joan's big date.

"I had *such* a good time," Joan said in a dreamy voice. She sounded as though she couldn't believe it. "When he picked me up, he looked different than he usually does. Really cool."

"What was he wearing?"

Joan didn't have to think very hard. She seemed to have memorized his clothing. "A blue-and white-striped polo shirt, black pants, a jean jacket, and high tops—with red shoelaces. And he had done something different to his hair, slicked it back or something. He looked *so* great."

"Where did you go?" Kim was getting a kick out of Joan's excitement.

"We were supposed to go to the movies, but it was so nice outside that we went to the board-walk and just hung out instead. He took me to this seafood place, and we had fried fish cakes and corn on the cob. It all comes in this great paper box so you can go out on the boardwalk and eat it there. I was really nervous at first, but he was so nice I forgot all about it. After that, we ended up just walking around and talking."

"And then?" Kim persisted, smiling mischie-vously.

Joan leaned over to whisper in Kim's ear. "He kissed me when we got to my house!" she ex-claimed. "I nearly died! I didn't know what to do."

"But you figured it out, right?"

"It does sort of come naturally," Joan admit-ted with a hint of a blush on her cheeks. "Should I have let him?" she murmured.

"Did you want him to kiss you?"

Joan's cheeks got even redder. "Yes," she admitted.

"Then you did the right thing," Kim said, a touch of envy in her voice. The last time she'd been kissed seemed like ages ago.

"Now all we've got to do is find someone for you," Joan said unexpectedly.

"Me?" Now Kim felt herself getting red.

"Yes, you. Jeff asked me out again, and Maria has Peter, so now we've got to fix you up with somebody."

Kim couldn't believe what she was hearing. All the things she had been saying to Joan were suddenly being said to her. It was as though they had switched personalities.

"I'm not really looking at the moment," Kim said weakly. With a sinking feeling, she realized that she was saying just what Joan used to say.

"There must be somebody," Joan went on persistently. The way she said it made it sound more like a question than a statement.

"Nope," Kim replied, sighing. "The only people I meet are jerks like Rick."

Her voice must have quivered when she said his name, because Joan gave her a strange look. "You really like him, don't you?" Joan asked quietly.

"No, I don't," Kim declared, trying to sound as though she meant it. "Definitely not." Still, she didn't want to close the subject completely. She needed to talk about it with somebody.

Joan continued to stare at her thoughtfully. "I don't think you really mean it. You don't sound as if you do. You *do* like him, don't you?"

That was all the prodding Kim needed for everything to spill out. "I'm so mixed up," she admitted. As she spoke, however, two boys got on the bus and took the seat right in front of them. "Let's go sit in the back," Kim whispered between gritted teeth.

They got up and moved to two seats in the rear of the bus where there would be more privacy. As soon as they sat down, Kim told Joan everything—about her first impression of Rick, about their collision at Mrs. Garcia's and how rude she had been, and about their meeting at Peabody's and how rude he had been. She wound up confessing that Rick was on her mind more than ever, even though she thought she hated him. "I don't know how I feel about him, Joan. What do you think of him?" Kim finally asked.

"I hardly know him," Joan admitted. "But I know he's had a pretty rough life." Even though she hadn't come out and said it, Kim knew that Joan was referring to the fact that his parents had died. "He's probably a pretty nice guy," Joan continued. "Look, you're going to be seeing him at the wedding, right?" Kim nodded. "Then just be yourself, and see what happens."

"I'm also going to see him the week before the wedding, not to mention at school," Kim said with a frown. "My mother just announced there's going to be a family dinner two weeks from Sunday. Everyone in Max's family and ours is going."

"What are you going to wear?" Joan asked immediately.

"*Wear?*" Kim demanded. "What am I going to *say?* The last time I saw him he turned his back on me."

"Forget about that," Joan said, trying to sound positive. "How many people are going to be at the dinner?"

"I'm not sure. About twenty or so. Both families have a lot of relatives who live here in Santa Barbara."

Joan thought the situation over. "You have to be extra nice to him," she said slowly. "Show some class. Show him that you're not petty. You can't make a scene in front of all those people, right?"

Kim glumly nodded her head in agreement.

"You don't know it yet, but you really like him," Joan continued. Kim looked at her in astonishment. "This is the perfect opportunity to get to know him. At least give him a chance. OK?"

Kim looked at her doubtfully. "Well, I'm not going to be rude again," she replied, glancing out the bus window. "But I don't see why—" Suddenly her mouth fell open. "This is our stop!" she exclaimed, reaching up to stop the bus. They had been talking so much they almost missed it.

After a breathless exit, they continued their conversation as they walked down Dolores Street to Mrs. Garcia's.

"About what I was saying before," Joan said, stopping in the middle of the sidewalk to emphasize her point. "I think you should give him a chance."

Kim kept walking. She was getting a little tired of Joan's cheerful advice. "I *gave* him a chance at Peabody's, and look how that turned out. It was a complete disaster."

Joan dropped the subject, obviously disappointed that she couldn't get through to Kim. Kim, on the other hand, knew Joan was right, but she was too stubborn to admit it. They continued in silence until they reached the dressmaker's house.

Kim introduced Joan to Mrs. Garcia, then they sat and waited as she adjusted Anne's flower-girl dress. It didn't need many alterations. Little Anne looked just as adorable as she had before, and Joan beamed when she saw her.

Then Mrs. Garcia beckoned Kim inside the dressing room. Kim followed reluctantly.

"Where are Spring and Elaine?" she asked as she stepped into her dress.

"They called. They're coming later," Mrs. Garcia said, looking her over. It seemed as though she had a million pins clasped between her teeth. "It's just you and the little one right now."

Kim's heart suddenly skipped a beat. What if Rick was coming to pick up Anne, as he had before? She hadn't even considered it. He was the last person in the world she wanted to see just then. *Especially in this horrible dress*, she thought as she glanced into the full-length mirror. A pensive frown marred Kim's pretty face.

It was hopeless, Kim decided. Although the bodice of the dress didn't look too bad now, and the lace collar did look very elegant, the skirt still stuck out from her hips, making her feel enormous. The material seemed to bunch up no matter what Mrs. Garcia did. *I look like the Jolly Pink Giant*, Kim thought in disgust.

Just then Kim heard Joan's voice from the other side of the curtain separating the dressing room from the living room. "Is it OK if I come and see?" she asked.

"Come on in," Kim said. She was relieved that she wouldn't have to parade around the living room in her dress—especially if Rick might show up at any minute to pick up Anne. But Kim knew it was a waste of time to feel relieved. Rick was going to see how stupid she looked at the wedding, and so would everyone else. For a moment Kim wished Vicki and Max had never met.

Joan brushed the curtain aside and stepped into the dressing room. "It's really cute," she said, not sounding too convinced. Her eyes seemed to be glued to the waistline.

Mrs. Garcia left the dressing room to get a tape measure and Kim turned to Joan. "I don't have the right body for this dress," she confessed miserably.

Joan continued staring at her friend. "May I make a suggestion?" she finally asked.

Kim shot her a look that seemed to say "why bother." "Go ahead," Kim said in a listless tone.

Mrs. Garcia came back just as Joan began to speak. "There's something that's not quite right about the waistline," Joan said slowly, trying to sound diplomatic. "Shouldn't it be a little higher?"

"It's a dropped waistline," Kim replied, rolling her eyes.

"Oh, right." Joan blushed a little at sounding so naive. Yet she stubbornly refused to give up. "Maybe it's the gathers then. Maybe the reason the dress makes you look so boxy is that the gathers aren't hitting your hips in the right place."

Kim noticed that Mrs. Garcia was knitting her brow, but to her amazement, the dressmaker seemed to agree with Joan. "Maybe we should go for a slightly straighter line," Mrs. Garcia said, taking a pin from between her teeth.

Even though it was still hard to visualize what the dress would look like from the pinned adjustments, Kim had to agree with Joan. The dress had to look a little better. A tiny ray of hope ran through her.

Kim changed back into her street clothes and was just leaving the dressing room when there was a knock at the front door.

She froze in her tracks and cursed her luck. *Why couldn't we have gotten out of here before Rick arrived?* she asked silently. Her hands suddenly felt clammy at the thought of seeing him.

To her surprise, when Mrs. Garcia opened the door, it wasn't Rick at all. It was his uncle George who had come to pick Anne up. He stopped to chat with them for a minute, and just before he and Anne left, he told Kim he'd see her soon—at the family dinner party. Kim smiled wanly.

After they left, Kim felt confused. As much as she hated to admit it, she was almost disappointed that Rick hadn't shown up. What did this mean? she wondered. Could Joan be right? She couldn't possibly be falling in love with him, could she?

# Chapter Seven

The prewedding family dinner was being held at the Talmadge Country Club. The Talmadge was the oldest club in town, and Kim knew it was considered the fanciest. She took special care getting dressed that night. She had selected a full, black cotton skirt, a peach, raw-silk blouse, and her good pearl necklace. But Kim wasn't only dressing for the Talmadge. In the back of her mind, she knew she was dressing for Rick, too. Despite her nervousness, she was determined to get to know him that night.

Her father drove the four of them to the club. It seemed funny to Kim to have her whole family in the car together; she could barely remember the last time they'd gone anywhere as a group like that. It felt good until she thought about Vicki getting married and moving away, then depression set in again. She looked over at her sister who looked very content and very happy. With an effort, Kim tried to feel the same way for her sake.

The country club was all lit up when they arrived, and a uniformed doorman helped them out of the car at the entrance. Inside, they went through the plush lobby to the private dining room that had been reserved for the party.

At the far end of the room there was a long table that had been set for dinner. The tablecloth was white with deep red embroidery around the hem; the red matched the exotic flowers floating in shallow bowls that were placed at intervals along the length of the table. There was a bar by the door, and some small chairs and couches. The place had a faintly musty smell, almost like that in a library, but Kim decided it was very elegant.

She quickly searched the room for Rick, but he wasn't there yet. She wasn't sure how she felt about not seeing him. On one hand, she worried that he wasn't coming, but at the same time she dreaded the awkward hellos they would probably exchange. Then it occurred to her that he *had* to come. She finally decided to just relax and prepare herself for his arrival.

She got a cup of fruit punch from the bar and walked over to a window seat. Sitting down on a red velvet cushion, she crossed her legs and struck what she thought was a sophisticated pose. Nobody seemed to notice.

After a while her mother wandered by and looked at her appraisingly. It almost seemed as though her mother didn't recognize her. "You look so pretty tonight, sweetie," she said. "You look very—grown-up." Her mother seemed as if she were about to cry. "Both my girls grew up so fast," she murmured, and shook her head.

"Oh, Mom," Kim said. She stood up and gave her mother a big hug.

"Honey," Mrs. Sommers continued once she had collected herself, "why don't you say hello to Max's mother. She was asking me about you."

"Sure, Mom," Kim replied and gave her another quick hug. She was about to leave when her mother touched her on the elbow. "Now remember, dear," she said in a stage whisper. "Stand up nice and straight."

Kim bristled. Why did her mother have to spoil things by reminding her that she was a giant? Looking around the room didn't make her feel any better, either—Max had the shortest relatives she had ever seen.

After greeting Max's mother, Kim sampled some of the fishy-smelling hors d'oeuvres that were being passed around. She quickly decided that they were awful. To wash the taste out of her mouth, she went to the end of the bar and asked for a ginger ale. Just then, Rick and his uncle George entered the room right beside her.

"Hi, little lady," Mr. Wheeler said to her immediately. Rick's uncle was originally from Texas and still had a heavy western drawl. The top of his head was very bald and very sunburned.

Kim froze. Rick was standing barely three feet in front of her. What was she supposed to do now? "Hi," she said, looking Rick's uncle in the eye. "It's nice to see you again, Mr. Wheeler." The funny thing was, she didn't feel as nervous as she thought she would.

"Do you know my nephew Rick?" Mr. Wheeler boomed.

Kim and Rick's eyes locked in mutual embarrassment. His brown eyes looked different from the way they usually did, Kim observed. They looked warmer, almost apologetic—not so icy as they had the time she had seen him at Peabody's.

"We've already met, Uncle George," Rick said, breaking the silence. His voice seemed rather unsteady. "Hi," he said to Kim gravely, then he looked down at the floor.

"Hello, Rick," Kim replied. His shyness was catching.

Mr. Wheeler didn't seem to notice their embarrassment, or at least he pretended not to. "I've got to go say hello to everyone," he announced. "It looks like supper's about ready." With that, he made a beeline for Vicki and Max, who were at the center of a cluster of relatives. Kim and Rick were left standing together, looking at each other uncomfortably.

Kim felt tongue-tied. And she thought that Rick should start the conversation. She remembered the last time she had taken the initiative—and the disastrous results. Now it was his turn.

Rick seemed to understand. "Well," he began and cleared his throat.

He was about to continue when a waiter walked into the room. "Ladies and gentlemen," the waiter announced, "dinner is served."

Rick looked at Kim with a funny expression—sort of a cross between relief and disappointment—and mumbled something she couldn't quite hear. Everyone in the room had started to move toward the long dinner table. "Um, see you," he finally said.

"See you," Kim echoed, disappointed. *That's it?* she wondered. *He's not going to say anything else?* It seemed just then as though they were never going to get the chance to have a decent conversation.

At the table Kim scanned the place cards for

the one with her name on it. When she found it, she stood behind her chair and looked down the table. Rick was on the opposite side and so far away that it would have been impossible to talk to him. Their eyes locked for an instant. Then, just as quickly, they looked away.

With a barely disguised sigh, Kim glanced around to see with whom she had been seated. To her right was her eight-year-old cousin Teddy, who was going to be the ring bearer at the wedding. The thought of switching Teddy's place card with Rick's flickered through her mind, but she knew it was too late. She was stuck.

Directly across the table from Kim was her mother. Automatically, Kim adjusted her posture, pulling her shoulders back. She didn't want her mom motioning to her all through dinner to sit up straight.

Kim's aunt Rose was seated to her left. At least there was somebody nearby that she could talk to, Kim thought. Even though her aunt Rose was nearly fifty, she always acted much younger, and she tried to keep up with all the latest things. Sometimes Kim thought she tried a little too hard, but still she was neat. Kim could talk to her. In fact, every Christmas for the past few years, her aunt had taken her aside and they had had a long, heart-to-heart talk. It was a nice tradition, and it made Kim look forward to the holiday all the more.

"So how's my favorite niece?" her aunt asked immediately after they were seated.

"I'm fine, Aunt Rose," Kim replied. "How are you?"

"Fine. Just fine," the older woman replied enthusiastically. "I've been taking this aerobics class, and even though it's exhausting, I feel wonderful."

"It sounds great," Kim said. Pointing to a tiny lacquered peacock pinned on her aunt Rose's collar, she added, "That's a neat pin." Her aunt always seemed to find the most un- usual clothes and jewelry.

"Why don't you have it," her aunt Rose said, unfastening the pin and handing it to Kim.

"Oh, no. It's beautiful, but you should keep it," Kim replied. She was surprised even though her aunt had a reputation for being generous.

"Nonsense, I want you to have it. It's probably too flashy for me, anyway," her aunt protested. "Your uncle Carl gave it to me," she said matter- of-factly. Carl had been her first husband, and Kim's aunt Rose had been married two more times since their divorce. All of her marriages had ended in divorce, which Kim never really understood. Her aunt had always seemed like a wonderful person to her.

"Thank you. It's very pretty," Kim said, examining the pin with delight. "I don't know if it goes with my outfit tonight, though."

"Then keep it for another time," her aunt said with a smile. She shook her napkin out, placed it in her lap, and leaned over to Kim with a confidential look in her eyes.

"So," Kim's aunt said conspiratorially, "what's new in your life? Are you dating anyone special?" There was no beating around the bush with her aunt, Kim remembered with a sinking feeling. She always got straight to the point.

"No, I'm not seeing anyone," Kim replied, staring down at her plate. She almost said "not yet," but she caught herself just in time. A quick glance down the table satisfied her that Rick couldn't hear them. He was too involved in his conversation with Max.

"I'm not seeing anyone, either." Aunt Rose sighed. A waiter appeared behind them and put salad plates on the table.

As Kim inspected the salad, her eyes fell on the place setting with dismay. There were so many forks laid out that she had no idea which one to use. Her eyes darted over to her aunt, who picked up the fork farthest from her plate. Kim tentatively followed her example.

"It's getting harder and harder to find good

men," her aunt Rose continued, taking a dainty bite of salad. "Mmm, this is good," she interrupted herself a moment later. "You have to be on the lookout for the right man all the time," she added with a twinkle in her eye. "He could be out there anywhere. Even here."

Kim didn't like the turn the conversation was taking, and her aunt sensed her uneasiness. "Pretty slim pickings tonight," the older woman confessed with a giggle. Kim tried to force a smile. Then her aunt leaned over to whisper. "Except maybe over there," she murmured. Her gaze moved down the table to settle on Rick.

Kim must have turned the same shade of red as her aunt's dress, for suddenly her mother shot her a warning look. "Don't eat too fast," she mouthed at her daughter.

Kim gave her mother a helpless look. The dinner was turning into a nightmare, and there was nothing Kim could do. Kim's aunt, however, must have realized that she had struck a nerve. She changed the subject immediately and started describing a cruise she had just taken down to Mexico. Of course, she had met several interesting men on board, all of whom she described in elaborate detail.

Kim nodded her head politely as her aunt's story unfolded, but try as she might, she couldn't keep her mind on it. She had the distinct feeling that someone was looking at her. Glancing away from her aunt Rose for just a second, she sneaked a peek down the table. Sure enough, Rick was staring at her. The minute their eyes met, he looked away.

Kim's heart fluttered excitedly, and throughout the rest of the meal, she glanced now and then in his direction. He looked very handsome in his blue blazer and gray slacks, and she realized that it was the first time she'd seen him wearing anything but jeans.

Her aunt's monologue continued, but Kim was only half listening, and she had barely touched the roast beef that had been placed in front of her. The little looks Rick kept shooting her—looks of apology, of friendship—made her so happy that she lost her appetite.

Her thoughts, and her aunt Rose's stories, were finally interrupted by the sound of a spoon tapping against a water glass. Kim looked down the table and saw Max's father rise and hold up his glass to make a toast. The table fell silent.

"There are few occasions in life as good as this," Mr. Wheeler began with a big toothy grin. "A toast to the future happiness of my son Max and his beautiful bride-to-be." Kim glanced over at Vicki, who managed to blush politely.

"Hear, hear," a couple of people said, and everyone clinked glasses.

"The future of every family lies in its young people," Mr. Wheeler continued. He was so wound up that it seemed as though he would never sit down. "I hope it won't be long until we're together again, toasting some other young couple." He paused theatrically and scanned the table. "Like Rick here," he said. Rick grimaced in embarrassment. Mr. Wheeler's gaze traveled down the table to Kim. She braced herself for what was coming.

"Or maybe Kim there," his voice boomed. "Wouldn't they make a fine couple?" He chuckled politely. Kim felt a few relatives turning their eyes on her. She wanted to die of embarrassment.

Everyone clinked glasses again as Kim burned with humiliation. She had barely met Rick, and now his uncle was already marrying them off. Her eyes remained focused on the bowl of flowers in front of her. She couldn't bear to look down the table at Rick. All she really wanted to do was go to the ladies' room and hide for the rest of the night.

Her aunt seemed to understand her discomfort and patted Kim's knee under the table. "Don't mind George," she said in a low voice. "I've known him for many years, and he doesn't have a mean bone in his body. That's just his way."

Kim forced herself to act nonchalant. "I just

feel a little silly," she confessed. She hoped she wasn't still blushing, but she felt awfully warm. Against her will, she glanced over at Rick. He continued to stare at his uncle George with an air of disbelief.

The dinner ended with chocolate mousse, which Kim didn't even touch, despite a sharp look from her mother. Her appetite had completely vanished. Her aunt tried to keep the conversation going, but Kim couldn't concentrate at all. She had been hoping to talk to Rick after dinner, but now she feared that if she did, everyone would stare at them.

When the coffee was brought out on a cart at the other end of the room, everyone got up from the table. Kim edged her way over, sticking close to her aunt Rose. Then, out of the corner of her eye, she saw Rick approaching them.

"Can I talk to you for a minute?" he asked shyly.

Her aunt gave her a slight nudge and then disappeared. "Sure," Kim replied. Her heart was pounding.

She followed him to an empty corner, and he glanced over his shoulder to make sure they had some privacy before he spoke. "I'm sorry about what my uncle said," he murmured apologetically. "That was way out of line."

"It's OK," Kim replied. Being alone with him

almost gave her goose bumps. At the same time she wished her entire family wasn't just a few yards away.

"And I'm sorry about that day at Peabody's—" Rick continued awkwardly, but his sentence was interrupted. Little Anne had spotted him and run over.

"Ricky, can I have a horsie ride?" she asked. Ordinarily, Kim would have been crushed at being interrupted, but Anne was so cute that she didn't mind. She enjoyed seeing how well the two of them got along. It made Rick even more attractive to her.

Rick looked at her sheepishly, but at the same time he seemed relieved to be interrupted. "All right," he said to Anne as he hoisted her up on his shoulders. He turned to Kim. "I wish I could offer you a ride home or something," he said. Kim couldn't believe how warm his voice sounded. "I can't, though," he said. "I've got a full car."

Kim smiled, thrilled at even being asked. "Some other time," she managed to say, trying to be super casual.

"I'm going to hold you to that promise," Rick replied with a grin. Then he trotted off with Anne bouncing merrily on his shoulders.

Kim watched them gallop off across the room as she walked back to her table. Then Rick's aunt said something to him, and he made Anne get down. They both looked rather embarrassed.

Kim took a sip of coffee. All at once everything seemed different. Rick had said just enough, with just the right words, to make her feel like a new person. She had to talk to Maria and Joan right away.

# Chapter Eight

The phone rang twice before anyone answered it. Finally someone picked it up, and Kim recognized Andy's squeaky voice.

"Hi, Andy, it's Kim," she said. "Is Joanie there?"

"No, she's got a *date* tonight," Andy said in a disgusted tone. Joan's ten-year-old brother could be so obnoxious sometimes. "Big deal," he added.

Kim sighed. "Tell her to call me, OK?"

"Sure," Andy said. "If I can find her when she's not making goo-goo eyes at that *boy*."

Kim hung up the phone feeling terribly disappointed. Maria hadn't been home, either—she was out on the boardwalk with Peter. Kim plopped down on her bed and kicked her shoes off. She had to tell somebody about what had happened with Rick at the family dinner. But who? "What should I do?" she asked, looking up at the ceiling. No one answered.

Frustrated, she pulled off her black skirt and peach blouse and changed into her nightshirt. After brushing her teeth and washing her face, she got into bed and turned out the light. Rick's face filled her mind. She thought she'd never get to sleep, but finally she did.

Kim's chance to talk to somebody about Rick came the following afternoon. Kim passed Maria a note in study hall asking if she wanted to play tennis after school, and Maria passed back a note saying she did.

To Kim's relief, Maria seemed to be in a good mood. As they walked to the public tennis courts, Kim hesitated before deciding not to ask how Peter was. She thought she'd better wait for the right moment. Besides, there were more important things she wanted to discuss. When they reached the courts, Kim led Maria over to a bench and sat her down.

"I want to ask you something," she began tentatively.

"Shoot," Maria said, reaching into her bag for her sweatband.

"What do you think of Rick Stone? Really."

Maria looked kind of surprised—and embarrassed at the same time. "I feel guilty," she confessed. "I was so rude to him at Peabody's. It was partly my bad mood and partly for your sake."

"My sake?" Kim asked.

"Didn't he make that rude comment about you at the basketball game?" Maria asked, tucking her hair under the sweatband. "Saying you were Kim Kong, or something like that?"

Kim winced at the recollection. "That was Whiz O'Neal," she muttered.

"Oh," Maria said. "Well, you hate Rick, anyway, don't you?" When Kim didn't reply, she repeated her question. "Don't you?" Suddenly she stared at Kim, studying her expression until she figured it out. "Oh, no," Maria said with a slight gasp. "You *do* like him."

"Well, kind of," Kim admitted in a small voice.

"That's—that's great," Maria sputtered. She was obviously surprised. "He *is* cute."

"He is kind of nice, isn't he?" Kim agreed. Then she turned and faced Maria squarely. "I was afraid you wouldn't think it was such a good idea."

"I think it's terrific, but what happened?" Maria asked. "What changed your mind?"

Kim related everything that happened at the family dinner in complete detail. She even revealed what Rick's uncle George had said in his toast.

"That sounds like one of my uncles," Maria remarked sympathetically.

"So, what do I do now?" Kim asked urgently. She realized that it was the kind of question Joan would ask. In fact, she was beginning to sound more and more like Joan every day.

"Well, at least you don't have to worry about when you'll see him again," Maria said. "With the wedding so close, you'll be seeing a lot of him at all the dinners and rehearsals."

"That's true," Kim replied, feeling a little uneasy at the thought.

"You just have to act cool and not be too forward," Maria said. She took her tennis racket out of her bag. "Want to play some tennis while we talk?"

"OK," Kim agreed. There wasn't anyone on either side of their court, so they had some privacy. Kim was glad because she still had so many questions she needed answers to. Maria's words kept echoing in her ears: "You'll be seeing a lot of him."

They took their places on opposite sides of the net, and Maria served the ball neatly across the court. "How's Vicki doing?" she asked.

"Pretty well," Kim said, struggling to return the ball. "I don't want to play a game, OK? Let's just rally."

"OK," Maria agreed, easily returning Kim's shot. "So, is Vicki nervous?" she continued.

"I don't know. I never get the chance to talk to her anymore. She's so busy all the time," Kim grunted, swinging her racket. Tennis came much easier to Maria than to Kim. "She does manage to pull everything together when she has to, though," Kim continued, puffing. "I'm sure the wedding will be fine. She looked really beautiful at the dinner last night."

"I can't believe the wedding is this weekend," Maria commented. "It seems as though you just told us about it yesterday."

"Me, neither," Kim agreed. "Oh, by the way. Can I stay over at your house the night before? My grandparents are coming to stay with us, and they're going to sleep in my room."

"Sure," Maria replied. "I thought you said your grandparents were at the dinner."

"Those were my other grandparents, on my father's side. My mom's parents won't be here until Friday afternoon."

"I would love to have been at that dinner," Maria said. "Just to see you and Rick together," she said, teasing her friend.

95

At that, Kim smacked the ball into the net, and it dribbled back to her, bouncing against her shoes. "It's not a joke, Maria. I'm serious," she said. "Rick really has me confused." Kim bent over and picked up the ball, hitting it into the net again. "I guess I'm not really in the mood for tennis," she confessed.

"That's all right," Maria said quickly. "I'm not, either. You need to talk about Rick more, don't you?"

Kim nodded her head, feeling a little foolish. "I really think I'm in love."

"Let's hope so," Maria said. "Now that Joan seems to be getting serious about Jeff—"

"She's never home," Kim interjected. "She doesn't even return my calls."

"She's really busy," Maria replied soothingly. She and Kim walked off the court and over to the bench where their things were. "Besides Jeff and school and band practice, she has gymnastics every day."

"I know, but I just feel like she's deserted me. Like you both have," she added in a tiny, hurt voice.

"Oh, Kimmie. You're my best friend," Maria said in a choked voice. She put her arm around Kim's shoulder. "I'd never do that to you."

Kim blinked back a tear. "I know," she said.

"I guess I'm just being dumb. It's just that this whole thing's got me so upset."

"It's really simple," Maria reassured her. "Just let it happen naturally. I know it will work out. I've got a good feeling about you and Rick." She dumped her racket and sweatband into her bag. "Let's go get a soda. My treat."

As Kim followed Maria across the street to the grocery store on the corner, she thought it was the right time to ask Maria about Peter. From the way Maria acted, things must be back to normal. "How's Peter?" Kim asked casually, swinging her bag.

"Oh, fine," Maria said airily. "We made up the other day." Her brown eyes glowed at the memory. "Or maybe I should say *I* made up. It was really my fault, anyway. I was upset about other stuff, and I took it out on Peter."

"What did you say to him?" Kim asked, intrigued.

"Well, it's kind of personal." Maria grinned. "We went down to the boardwalk to watch the sunset, and I told him what a dope I was. Then it got a little mushy."

"Oh, yeah?" Kim replied. It all sounded so romantic.

Maria read her thoughts. "I highly recommend the boardwalk at sundown for a romantic setting," she said. "Maybe you should try to get Rick to take you down there."

"I wish I could," Kim said.

"You will someday," Maria promised.

Kim finally caught up with Joan two days later at band practice. Joan looked extremely apologetic. "I'm really sorry I haven't had a chance to talk to you," she said. "Maria called and told me how upset you were."

Kim felt slightly embarrassed. What she had wanted to talk about wasn't exactly a matter of life and death. "That's OK," she murmured. "You know, you were right about Rick," she confessed.

Joan stared at Kim. "Did he ask you out?" she asked in an excited voice.

"Not exactly," Kim admitted. "But he was super friendly when I saw him in the hall yesterday." Kim thought briefly back to the day before, and the heart-melting smile Rick had flashed at her as he'd passed her outside the cafeteria. He didn't say a word, but he didn't have to.

Suddenly a whistle sounded, signaling the band members that it was now time to take their places. Mr. Banfield, the band leader, was still dissatisfied with their formations, so they were doing marching drills that afternoon—without their instruments. Kim was glad. Since she and Joan were positioned side by side, they could continue their conversation. They took their places.

"When are you seeing him again?" Joan asked. She seemed almost as excited as Kim was.

"Tomorrow night at the rehearsal dinner."

"Oh, gosh!" Joan exclaimed. "The wedding is this weekend?"

"It's this Saturday," Kim replied. "Where have you been?"

Joan leaned over to whisper in her ear. "I've been kind of preoccupied," she said meaningfully. "Things have been going really well with Jeff." Mr. Banfield blew his whistle twice, and they started marching around the football field.

"That's so great!" Kim said, trying to get in step. *Maybe some of Joan's luck will rub off on me,* she hoped.

"Thanks." Joan smiled shyly. "By the way," she continued, "why is the rehearsal dinner tomorrow? Isn't it usually the night before the wedding?"

"There's some huge party at the hotel on Friday night," Kim explained. "Vicki decided to switch the whole thing to Thursday instead of trying to find some other place for us to have dinner after the rehearsal."

Joan was about to say something else when Mr. Banfield's voice rang out from the front of the line. "Miss Sommers," he yelled at Kim.

"Yes," she piped up in a guilty voice.

"Please stop your conversation. It's no wonder this band can't march decently when you people aren't even paying attention."

"Yes, sir," Kim replied meekly. Mr. Banfield blew his whistle twice, and the team resumed marching. Kim cocked her head at Joan and made a face, but she kept her mouth shut. She didn't want to wind up in detention. Still, there was one more thing she had to ask Joan. When Mr. Banfield turned his back, she turned to Joan. "Can you come to my house this afternoon?" she whispered as quickly as possible.

Joan gave Kim a questioning look, and nodded her head just as Mr. Banfield whirled around to see who was whispering. Kim tried to act as innocent as possible. Fortunately, it worked.

Kim had asked Joan to come over because her mother was supposed to have picked up her finished bridesmaid dress that afternoon, and Kim wanted to model it for her friend. The last time Kim had tried the dress on, Joan had brought her good luck. If she had needed the luck then, Kim needed it even more now.

"Is the dress here?" Kim asked her mother when they walked in the door.

"Yes, dear," Mrs. Sommers said absently. She was sitting in front of the sewing machine working on her own outfit for the wedding. An experienced seamstress herself, Kim's mother had decided to make her dress. She was just putting the finishing touches on the ice-blue gown. "It's upstairs in your closet."

"Your dress is coming along great, Mom," Kim said. Then she practically dragged Joan up the stairs to her room. Flinging open her closet door, she saw the dress hanging up wrapped in a plastic bag.

"I hope it turned out OK," she said as she tore the plastic off. She held it up in front of her, but that didn't help.

"Try it on," Joan urged.

Kim slipped into the dress, zipped it up, and then turned to Joan expectantly. From Joan's expression, she decided it must be a success. She glided over to her mirror.

Kim examined herself carefully, from every angle. "I can't believe it," she exclaimed, sighing with relief. "It looks fantastic."

The small adjustments Joan had suggested seemed to make all the difference in the world.

Instead of hanging down limply like a sack, the dress actually made her look good. "I owe it all to you," Kim said as she gave Joan a hug.

"Oh, no," Joan scoffed, "I hardly did anything. You're the one who looks great in it."

Kim glowed with pride. Suddenly everything seemed to be coming together. Her worries about how she would look had evaporated, and things with Rick seemed promising. It was too good to be true, she decided as she spun around the room in delight.

# Chapter Nine

The Palms Hotel shone under the sunny, late-afternoon sky as Kim, along with Vicki and Max, arrived for the wedding rehearsal on Thursday. As Max drove them over, Kim tapped her feet in the backseat, full of anticipation. Not only would Vicki and Max's closest friends be at the rehearsal, but so would Rick. And following the rehearsal, there was the dinner for the wedding party. Kim was determined to be as charming and sophisticated as she could possibly be.

Miss Phipps, the wedding coordinator, met them in the parking lot. Her arms were loaded down with notebooks and a clipboard, and a pair of wire-rim glasses were perched precariously on the end of her nose. Miss Phipps looked tired and harried.

"Don't you look lovely today," she said to Vicki automatically. "I have to talk to you in the office," she said. "There seems to be some confusion—" Suddenly she stopped and turned to Kim. "You are?" she asked, her pen poised above her clipboard.

"Kim Sommers," Kim said. "One of the bridesmaids."

"Ah, yes," Miss Phipps said, checking Kim's name off the list. "The rest of the wedding party is waiting by the gazebo," she said, gesturing grandly toward a stone staircase leading down to the enclosed garden where the wedding was to be held. "Please join them. We'll be right down."

As Kim descended the steps, she looked around in wonder. She had never been on the grounds of the Palms Hotel before, and she was very impressed. The place was fantastic—and very romantic. Instead of one main building, the hotel was made up of clusters of small bungalows, arranged on a hill surrounding a lush garden. Bordering the garden on one side was a long, kidney-shaped pond. An ivy-covered stone bridge seemed to grow over it.

The rest of the wedding party was standing under the gazebo at the far end of the garden.

Her eyes raked the group for Rick. Then she saw him, standing off to one side, talking to Elaine and Spring. When she got a little closer, he turned, and their eyes met for a second. Suddenly Kim felt very self-conscious about being the last to arrive. She wished Max had been on time.

Slightly hypnotized, Kim walked over to them. "Hi," she said, trying to keep her voice even.

"Hi, Kim," Elaine replied. In her purple jogging outfit, she didn't look anything like a maid of honor, Kim thought. She wasn't even wearing makeup.

Spring said hello, then tried to make introductions. "Do you two know each other?" she asked Kim and Rick innocently.

"We've met," Kim said with a smile. Her heart was racing. Somehow Rick looked different, but she couldn't quite figure out why. Then he ran his hand through his hair, and Kim realized what it was. "You got a haircut," she blurted out.

"You noticed," Rick said sheepishly. "I got scalped. It was my aunt's idea." Kim could tell he was teasing her a little. His eyes seemed just then to be a very deep shade of brown, and Kim remembered that Vicki had once said: "You can tell how he feels from his eyes." Kim wondered if eye color made any difference.

Miss Phipps reappeared with Vicki and Max and clapped her hands briskly to get everyone's attention. "All right," she said, pushing her glasses up on her nose. "I haven't got much time, so we'll have to rehearse as quickly as possible. Will the bridesmaids stand over here and the ushers over there," she said, pointing to opposite sides of the gazebo.

As soon as everyone was in place, Miss Phipps explained where they would assemble and how they would each walk in before the ceremony. Her short, clipped sentences sounded like gunfire. "She's like a drill sergeant," Spring whispered to Kim, giggling.

Then Miss Phipps looked at her clipboard and sized up the bridesmaids. "Ladies, I'm going to arrange you by height," she said. "These will be your places in the procession." Then she read off their names, starting with the little flower girl, Anne. To Kim's embarrassment, she was placed at the very end. *Naturally*, she thought. She was by far the tallest girl among them.

After Miss Phipps had arranged the boys in the same manner, she stood back and surveyed the ensemble. "You all look very nice," she said brusquely. "Now," she continued, "after the ceremony, the ushers, starting with the ring bearer, will walk over and offer their arms to the bridesmaids and escort them out. Then each couple will walk down the path to the bridge and wait there. All right, let's try it."

With that, she prodded little Anne and Teddy forward. The tiny couple walked slowly and solemnly, obviously trying very hard. The rest of the wedding party cracked up. They looked so adorable.

"The next couple, please," Miss Phipps prompted. Elaine and Greg, the best man, linked arms and were about to walk down the aisle. But as they turned, Elaine tripped over Greg's feet. Everybody cracked up again.

Everybody except Kim. By process of elimination, she realized that she would be paired up with Rick, who was the tallest boy there. He was standing directly opposite her. Kim felt excited but nervous at the same time. She was determined not to mess up.

"Now the next couple," Miss Phipps continued. She didn't find Elaine's stumbling very amusing.

Spring and her escort went next, and the minute they joined arms and looked at each other, they started to laugh and couldn't stop. Their laughter was contagious and even Kim found herself laughing, in spite of her nervousness.

"Now the final couple," Miss Phipps said grimly.

Kim noticed that Rick looked as nervous as she was, but with a start, he jerked forward and offered her his arm.

Kim linked her arm lightly through his, and a surge of electricity ran through her. She gave him a shy, self-conscious smile. He smiled back. As they walked down the path, the laughter from the rest of the group faded away, and they all seemed to be watching with interest.

"Excellent," Miss Phipps said. "That's all there is to it. You'll remain at the bridge for photographs immediately after the ceremony. Are there any questions?"

Nobody answered, so Miss Phipps went over to consult with Vicki and Max, who had been watching the proceedings from the lawn. Miss Phipps led them over to the gazebo, and ran through the ceremony with them.

Rick and Kim remained standing together by the bridge with the rest of the wedding party. Trying to be casual, Kim slipped her arm out of his and clasped her hands tightly behind her back. She tried to think of something to say, but her mind was a blank.

"Aren't they a cute couple?" she heard someone murmur behind her. She turned and saw Spring and Elaine staring at them.

Kim blushed to the roots of her hair. Rick must have heard it, too, because he shifted his feet awkwardly. "I feel so dumb," he confessed in a low voice.

"Me, too," Kim agreed. Secretly, she was thrilled. For the first time in her life, she didn't feel like a giant at all. Standing beside him, she felt normal. Spring was right, Kim decided. She and Rick *did* make a cute couple.

Miss Phipps finished rehearsing with Vicki and Max and got the whole group together again. "On Saturday, please be here no later than ten o'clock," she said. "The wedding will begin at eleven sharp, and we will need some time beforehand for pictures." She looked up, and the sun glinted on her glasses. Kim decided she wasn't really rude, just overworked. "That's all. Thank you for coming," Miss Phipps said. Then she walked briskly up the stairs.

Vicki called the bridesmaids together. "You guys were great," she said in a teasing tone. Then she became more serious. "I think we're going to have to meet here early to get dressed by ten," she added. "It's going to take me awhile."

"Definitely," Spring agreed. "What time do you want us to be here?"

"I'm planning to be here around eight-thirty," Vicki said. Her eyes automatically went to her watch. "Oh, no, I'm late!" she exclaimed. "The dinner tonight is at seven," she reminded them before she took off.

Kim's mind raced ahead to the rehearsal dinner that evening. She knew it was going to be a small group, just the wedding party, and she knew she'd finally get a chance to talk with Rick. She thought of the outfit she had laid out on her bed for the dinner. She was feeling very confident, and the feeling of Rick's arm touching hers lingered in her mind.

The rehearsal dinner was held in the main dining room at the hotel. Two tables had been pushed together for their party of twelve, and everyone she had seen earlier that day was there, except for little Teddy and Anne. Max's parents and Mr. and Mrs. Sommers were there as well.

"What a cute outfit," Spring said when she saw Kim.

"Thanks," Kim said modestly. She had bought the outfit—a stylish, royal-blue cotton sweater and tan linen pants—especially for the occasion. She had even bought a ribbon that matched the sweater to tie her hair back.

Her eyes darted around the table, looking for the person she had gotten so dressed up for. When she spotted him, and the empty chair beside him, her heart started to thump in anticipation.

As she had hoped, Max and Vicki took the two empty places at the head of the table, leaving the only vacant seat next to Rick. It was the opportunity Kim had been hoping for. Taking a deep breath, she slid into the chair next to him.

"Hi," he said immediately. He seemed more lively than he had been that afternoon. There was so much talking going on at the table that she had to strain to hear him, but despite the noise, she was happy. At least they could have a little privacy. She flashed him a smile. He looked very handsome with his short haircut.

"When you're in a wedding, you sure have to go to a lot of dinners," he remarked, obviously trying to get a conversation going.

Kim laughed in agreement. "When this is over, I'm going to need a whole new wardrobe—two sizes larger," she said lightly.

Rick smiled back. There was a long pause as if he were trying to think of something clever to say.

Kim broke the ice first. She was bursting with questions. Suddenly, there was so much she wanted to ask him. "How do you like Santa Barbara High?" she began boldly.

"It's OK," Rick replied with a pained expression. "It's kind of hard to get to know people there, though," he admitted.

"That just takes time," Kim interjected, guiltily recalling her own negative first impression of him.

"I know. But it's been a big adjustment going to a school with girls," Rick went on. "I was in an all-boys boarding school before."

"Oh, really?" Kim asked innocently, as if she knew nothing about his past.

"Yeah," Rick said uncomfortably, tapping his fork on the table. "I got sent there after my parents died." His brown eyes looked very sad. "If my aunt and uncle hadn't rescued me, I'd still be there."

Kim was moved by his honesty. "Boarding school must have been awful," she said sympathetically.

"The worst," Rick said, warming to the subject. "We had to get up at six-thirty in the morning, wash, and then clean up our rooms for inspection at seven."

"Ugh," Kim said. "*Six-thirty!*" Even though she was interested, her attention was getting sidetracked by the incredible brown of his eyes.

"It was the pits," Rick agreed. He stopped playing with his fork. "At least that's all behind me now." He let out a sigh of relief. "What about you?" he asked. "Have you lived here all your life?"

"Yes," Kim said, flattered by his curiosity. She wished her life had been more exotic. "There really isn't a lot to tell," she began. "We live in Lynnhaven, my parents and my sister and I—"

Kim paused for a moment. Her sadness about Vicki moving away swelled up inside her. "I'm really going to miss Vicki," she admitted.

"It's hard to say goodbye to people who are close to you," Rick said simply.

Kim swallowed in embarrassment. She knew he was talking about his parents, and she suddenly felt awfully selfish about missing Vicki, who was only moving away. At the same time, she was impressed by Rick's gentle honesty. It was so easy to talk to him.

Just then the main course was brought out— whole lobsters. The waiter handed them lobster bibs to tie around their necks, and Kim's heart sank momentarily. After all the trouble she had gone through to make sure she looked nice, she thought, now it was going to be all covered up. Still, she was relieved about one thing—she had had lobster before, and she knew the correct way to eat it. Rick had more difficulty, but he joked about his clumsiness, making her laugh.

Their conversation continued easily through the whole dinner. She told Rick all about how she and Maria and Joan had become friends, then they discussed school and certain teachers at length. By the time dessert was served, Kim felt that she was finally getting to know him. She couldn't believe how different he was from what she had first imagined.

As the coffee was being poured, Rick leaned over to her and asked a question that had been hovering in the air all night, unspoken. "Are you dating anyone?" he mumbled.

Kim took a sip of coffee before she answered. "Not really," she said casually, trying to sound popular but available at the same time.

Rick didn't say anything in response. His silence didn't bother Kim though, because she thought she knew the reason for it. Rick was just plain shy.

After dinner a series of toasts to the prospective bride and groom began. Although she was too shy to propose her own toast, Kim lifted her glass along with the others. Then, to her complete surprise, after the last toast, Rick clinked his glass with hers. "To you, Kim," he said in a low voice.

As she stared into his eyes, Kim forgot everything around her. Then and there, she knew she was in love.

# Chapter Ten

The day before the wedding arrived sunny and bright, and Kim sat at the breakfast table, toying with her food. An atmosphere of anticipation hung in the air.

"It better not rain tomorrow," Vicki muttered as she searched through the paper for the weather forecast.

"Don't worry, it won't," her mother said, glancing out the window at the cloudless sky. "I won't let it." She picked up a list that had been lying on the table and scanned it. "You're spending the night at Maria's tonight, right?" she asked Kim.

"Yes, ma'am," Kim replied. They had gone over where Kim would stay at least a million times already. "Maria invited Joanie, too. It's going to be kind of a pajama party. Then they're going to go to the wedding together tomorrow."

"That's nice," her mother replied, not really listening.

"What time are Grandma and Grandpa coming?" Kim asked.

Her mother flipped to another page of notes. "Their flight gets in tonight at six-thirty," she said. Her finger moved down the column of notes. "Did you clean up your room?"

"Yes, Mom," Kim groaned. Sometimes her mother made her feel as though she didn't have any sense.

"Good girl." Her mother made a check next to the words "Kim's room." Her pencil lingered over the next item. "Honey," she said to Vicki, "can you pick up your grandparents at the airport tonight?"

"Mother," Vicki protested, "I'm going to be at the spa all day. I don't know when I'll be done." Vicki was going to have a massage, facial, manicure—the works.

"Well, I don't have time, either," her mother said. "I have to pick up Martha and Bill at the train station," she said with a hint of dismay in her voice. "And your father has a late meeting. Please, couldn't you drop your dresses off at the hotel suite where you're going to change tomorrow? Then drop Kim at Maria's and go from there to the airport and pick up Grandma and Grandpa."

"But, Mom," Vicki began. But then she saw the look on her mother's face. "Anything you say," she said, forcing a smile. "It just better not rain," she added with a frown.

Vicki seemed to be glowing when they left on their errands that evening. Her day at the spa had been a success, Kim decided. Maybe getting married was worth all the trouble if you got to go somewhere and have someone make you look that good, she mused.

The first place they stopped was at the hotel. The suite where they would change for the wedding had a living room and a bedroom, in addition to the largest bathroom Kim had ever seen. After thoroughly inspecting the rooms and carefully hanging up their dresses, they headed for Maria's.

They didn't say much in the car, but Kim's mind was racing. It was the last day Vicki would be single, she thought, and probably the last time they'd be driving around together for a long time. It made her sad.

"Vicki," she began tentatively. Then she stopped. She didn't know how to put what she was feeling into words. "I'm really going to miss you," she managed to say.

"Oh, Kimmie," Vicki said, and a big tear ran down her cheek. "I'm going to miss you, too. I'm going to miss everything," she added with a sniffle. "How did you know what I was thinking?"

Kim shook her head mutely. She felt as if a part of her life were ending, a part she'd never appreciated enough.

Impulsively, Vicki pulled the car off the highway and onto a side street. Turning off the ignition, she swiveled in her seat to give Kim her full attention. "There's something I want to tell you," she said, clearing her throat. "I haven't been a very good sister to you lately," she confessed. "And I'm really sorry."

"No." Kim's eyes filled with tears. "I understand. You've been so busy. It's really OK."

"No, it isn't," Vicki said stubbornly. "I've been so wrapped up in myself and the wedding that I've been ignoring you completely." Vicki looked very guilty. "You know I didn't mean to, don't you? You know how special you are to me."

"I feel the same way," Kim replied softly. Vicki had finally come through for her.

"I almost feel as though I'm deserting you," Vicki went on. "I mean, once I'm gone, who's going to be on your side when you and Mom have an argument?" She smiled. "And who's going to give you advice on your love life?"

Kim couldn't hold the tears back any longer. Vicki let out a sob, too, and they hugged each other.

"Don't worry," Vicki said, sniffling loudly. "You can come visit us whenever you want. It's only a plane ticket, you know." She reached for a issue from the box on the dashboard. "I've been so proud of you lately," she continued. Taking Kim by the shoulders, she looked into her eyes. "You really impressed me with how mature you've become. Elaine even said something to me about it. You were so cool at all the parties and stuff."

"Thanks," Kim mumbled, wiping her eyes. "I guess I'm growing up," she said simply.

"I guess we both are," Vicki agreed with a sigh. "May I ask you something personal?" she almost whispered.

"Sure."

"You really do like Rick, don't you?"

Kim wasn't surprised that Vicki could tell. There were some things sisters just knew. Since their talk was so heart-to-heart, she had to be honest, so she nodded her head.

Vicki's eyes flashed. "I thought so. I was watching you two out of the corner of my eye at the dinner last night." The thought of it made her smile. "I think he's such a great guy," she went on. "He's had a rough time of it, though. He needs a lot of love." She studied Kim's face but didn't have any idea what she was hoping to find. "I think he likes you, too," Vicki finally said.

Kim's face lit up. "Did Max say anything to you?"

"I would never ask Max," Vicki said at once. "You know how guys are. And I didn't need to ask him, anyway. I can just tell."

"How?"

"You can tell by his eyes. I saw the way he was looking at you last night. He likes you, all right."

"Oh, Vicki," Kim exclaimed, giving her sister another hug. She had been dying for someone to reassure her that Rick really did like her.

"Anyway," Vicki said, dabbing at the corners of her eyes with a tissue, "my advice is *go* for it." She turned the key in the ignition and restarted the car. "Do you understand me?"

"I understand." Kim smiled.

They drove for a while in silence, then Vicki murmured, "Don't forget what I said. I'm always here for you. Even if I'm far away."

Kim gave Vicki's hand a squeeze in reply. She didn't say anything. She didn't have to.

As they continued on their way to Maria's,

Kim stared out the window at the palm trees flashing by. *A wonderful moment like this,* she thought, *doesn't come often in life.* She wanted to hold on to it.

"I want to hear everything," Maria said when she opened the door. "Every last detail." Her hair was wrapped in a towel, and she was carrying a large bowl of popcorn.

"Is Joanie here yet?" Kim asked as they made their way through the house. "I want her to hear it, too."

"She should be here any minute," Maria said as they entered her bedroom. The room was large and pink and dominated by a canopied bed covered with a pink- and blue-flowered spread. That night, however, something else took center stage—an enormous, red, heart-shaped balloon, hovering near the ceiling, with a tangle of red streamers hanging from it.

"I see Peter got you your valentine early," Kim said with a tinge of envy in her voice. She had forgotten all about Valentine's Day in the excitement of the wedding.

"It's not from Peter," Maria said softly, lowering her eyes. "It's from my dad. It just came."

"Oh," Kim mumbled uneasily.

Maria plopped down on the floor at the foot of her bed. "I was kind of embarrassed when it came," she confessed. "My mom was right there when I opened the card, and I think she got kind of depressed."

"Things haven't gotten any better, have they?" Kim murmured.

Maria shook her head. "There's definitely going to be a divorce," she said, sighing. She took a handful of popcorn and munched on it distractedly. "Sometimes I wish I were you, Kim," she said out of the blue.

"*Me?*" Kim gasped. Kim always thought Maria had everything. "You're the one who's always been Miss Perfect," Kim countered. "Why on earth would you want to be me?"

Maria let out a short laugh. "I'm far from being Miss Perfect. You're the one with the great family life," she said. "You have parents who love you and love each other. That's what's really important."

"Your parents still love you," Kim said. Maria didn't say anything. "I guess sometimes I do take it for granted, though," she admitted.

"Well, don't," Maria said. There was a short pause, then she got up and stretched, as if to stretch her feelings away. "Just be glad about it." She pulled the towel off her head and briskly began drying her hair with it.

"How's your mom doing?" Kim asked.

"Better, I guess. She seems to be getting used

to the idea of not being married anymore," Maria said, trying to sound positive. She began combing out her hair, yanking at the tangles. Just then the doorbell rang. They could hear Joan saying hello to Maria's mother downstairs. "Great, Joanie's finally here," Maria exclaimed. "Now we can really start the party."

A minute later Joan bustled into the room, carrying a dress bag containing her outfit for the wedding. When Kim saw her, she nearly did a double take. Joan had straightened her hair. Instead of her usual tight little curls, her hair now fell in soft, shiny waves. It was astounding how different she looked.

"I don't believe it," Maria said, her jaw dropping open.

"You look fantastic," Kim echoed.

Joan flipped her bag on the bed and nervously patted her hair. "You really think so?"

Maria nodded her head vigorously. "Where did you get it done?"

"At the mall. At Hair People," Joan replied, helping herself to a handful of popcorn. "But forget my hair," she said, turning to Kim expectantly. "I want to hear what happened with Rick last night. From the beginning," she emphasized.

Kim took a deep breath. "Well, I sat next to him at the dinner, and we talked for a long time."

"About what?" Maria said, munching on some popcorn.

"Just about each other. Our backgrounds, stuff like that." Kim paused thoughtfully. "I guess I really misjudged him. He's not a jerk at all."

"I told you so," Joan said at once, only to be silenced by a sharp look from Maria.

"He's been through a lot," Kim began.

"But with a little love . . ." Joan interrupted.

"Joan!" Maria exclaimed. "Let Kim tell it, all right?"

"Sorry," Joan murmured.

So Kim repeated everything they had talked about, finishing with his question and her answer about whether she was seeing anybody or not.

"Then what did he say?" Maria demanded.

"Nothing," Kim admitted. "He sort of went back to playing with his food. Do you think I said the wrong thing?"

"Maybe he just needs time to get up the nerve to ask you out," Maria suggested. "After that time he spent in a boys' boarding school, I'll bet he still doesn't feel comfortable around girls."

"Maria's right," Joan agreed. "I'll bet he asks you out soon. Maybe he'll ask you tomorrow at the wedding."

"I hope so," Kim said. Still, from the disappointed looks on their faces, Kim felt as though she had just told a joke and then forgotten the punch line. She felt a little foolish making such a big deal about nothing. "How are things going with Jeff?" she asked Joan, trying to move the subject away from her own dull love life.

"Just great," Joan grinned. "He's picking me up after the wedding, and we're going to go somewhere. It's a surprise, though. He won't tell me where."

"It *is* Valentine's Day tomorrow," Maria said, winking at Kim.

*And everyone's got a valentine except me,* Kim thought. But in the back of her mind, there was a ray of hope.

# Chapter Eleven

The day of the wedding began early for Kim. She got out of her sleeping bag at the foot of Maria's bed at seven o'clock and took a long, hot shower. Then she woke Joan and, after coaxing her to drink some orange juice, managed to get her up. They both dressed in silence. With a quick goodbye to the half-asleep Maria, Joan drove Kim to the Palms Hotel. "See you in a couple of hours," she called before she drove away.

Even then, Kim had barely noticed the overcast sky. It was so early in the morning that she just assumed it was haze and that it would burn off later on. It was only when she entered the hotel suite where the other bridesmaids and Vicki were changing that she realized how serious it was.

"I can't believe it. It's going to rain," Vicki was moaning. She collapsed on the bed, burying her face in her arms.

Kim stood in the doorway, speechless. This was not the welcome she expected. The suite looked like a disaster area. Vicki's gown was hanging on the closet door, and her veil, wrapped in tissue paper, lay over one of the dressers. The rest of the room was a jumble of makeup kits, tote bags, and hot curlers. A room-service cart with an urn of coffee and some doughnuts on it had been pushed against the wall. A cassette player was blaring.

At the sound of Vicki's wail, Spring emerged from the bathroom, carrying a mascara brush. "Now just stop that right now," she said to Vicki in a loud voice. "You don't want your eyes to be all puffy today, do you?"

Spring's tone of voice startled Vicki into silence, and she sat up on the bed. She looked at Kim desperately. "*What* am I going to do?" she asked.

"Just stay calm," Kim said, sitting down on the bed beside her. She reached over and turned the cassette player down. "It's not going to rain. It's just a little cloudy, that's all." She took Vicki's hand and gave it a squeeze.

This seemed to satisfy Vicki temporarily, and she carefully wiped her eyes with a tissue. "Is the hairdresser here yet?" she asked in a daze.

Elaine's voice came from the bathroom. "She's in here with me. We're all done now."

"You go next," Vicki said to Kim. "Has anyone heard the weather forecast?" she asked.

"It's not supposed to rain," Kim replied in what she hoped was a soothing tone. "Now, just try to relax. Put your feet up. I'll be really fast with the hairdresser."

The door to the suite opened, and Kim's mother burst in. "Aren't you two getting ready yet?" she demanded. In comparison to her two daughters, Mrs. Sommers looked immaculate. Her ice-blue dress had turned out beautifully— very chic and elegant.

"I just got here," Kim said defensively.

"What about your sister?"

"Vicki's afraid it's going to rain," Kim blurted out.

"If it rains, the ceremony will be in the ballroom," her mother said firmly. "Now stop worrying about it and get dressed," she commanded Vicki.

Vicki got off the bed, and just then Kim realized that it wasn't just the weather that was upsetting her sister. Vicki was scared stiff about getting married.

"Kim," her mother continued, "help your sister. Miss Phipps wants you girls to be ready for pictures in forty-five minutes." She glanced at her watch. "I have to find the florist. Your bouquets aren't here yet." Her mother paused in front of a mirror and quickly examined her appearance. "Do I look all right?" she asked.

"You look wonderful, Mom," Kim said, trying to reassure her.

"Help your sister," her mother repeated. "We only have about an hour and half until the ceremony. *Please.*" With that, she took off.

Elaine emerged from the bathroom in a silk kimono, her hair arranged elaborately on top of her head. "I can help Vicki," she told Kim. "You go in and get your hair fixed."

Kim went into the bathroom and found it to be just as chaotic as the bedroom. Makeup and curlers were scattered all over the counter. Standing by a chair in front of the mirror was her mother's hairdresser, Mrs. Carruthers, who had been hired to style all the girls' hair.

"We have to be quick," Mrs. Carruthers said. "I haven't even seen the bride yet."

Kim sat down meekly.

At first Mrs. Carruthers suggested piling Kim's long blond hair on top of her head, the way Elaine's was, but Kim objected. "It'll make me look too tall," she protested in a tiny voice. Mrs. Carruthers sort of chuckled, but she didn't argue about it. Instead, she pulled Kim's hair back into a French twist, fastened it with lots of pins, and then after spraying on a ton of hairspray, she stuck some baby's breath in it.

Kim was thrilled at how sophisticated it looked. When Spring came into the bathroom, she gasped. "You look fabulous!" she said. Kim could tell Spring was truly impressed. "Do you want some help with your makeup?" Spring offered.

Kim nodded shyly, and Spring whisked her out of the way as Mrs. Carruthers led Vicki into the bathroom.

Spring sat Kim down on the bed, and in a flash expertly made her up. Even though Spring put on much more makeup than Kim was accustomed to, the result was so subtle that Kim could hardly tell it was there. Her cheeks had a natural-looking rosy glow, and the deep green in her eyes had been brought out. "Wow," she murmured to Spring, "you should be a makeup artist."

"Thanks," Spring replied. "And now, I've got to do your sister. Let's both cross our fingers," she said as she disappeared into the bathroom.

Just then, Mrs. Wheeler and Anne arrived.

The little girl was dressed and ready and looked as cute as a button. "Kim, could you keep an eye on Annie?" Mrs. Wheeler asked. "I need someone to make sure she doesn't get dirty, while I see if Max needs any help."

As Kim changed into her dress, Anne darted around the room, peeking into shopping bags and makeup kits. Something about her dress itched her, and every now and then the little girl would scratch herself vigorously. Kim laughed in spite of herself.

Kim put on her dress, carefully smoothing it out. Then she stepped over to check her reflection in the mirror. Seeing it all together—the dress, her hair, and her makeup—sent a shiver of delight through her. Kim knew she looked her very best. *And that's pretty darn good*, Kim thought, smiling at her reflection.

A sudden knock on the door startled Kim, and she jumped away from the mirror. Since she had been specifically instructed not to let anyone see their dresses before the ceremony, Kim only opened the door a crack and peered out. A hotel bellboy was standing there, holding a huge box that had been wrapped in cellophane. "Your bouquets," he said.

"Oh, thanks," Kim said, sticking her hand through the door and pulling in the bouquets one by one. She wasn't sure if she was allowed to let the bellboy see her dress, but she didn't want to take any chances.

The bouquets smelled wonderful. The bridesmaids would be carrying a mass of ferns, sprinkled with freesia, baby's breath, and several other flowers she couldn't identify, while Vicki's bouquet was a mass of white roses that trailed down gracefully about a foot and a half.

Kim posed in front of the mirror holding the bridal bouquet, and a vision of Rick standing next to her flashed through her mind. Just then the bathroom door flew open, and Vicki emerged —she looked absolutely radiant. Kim quickly hid the bridal bouquet behind her back, then turned to face her sister. Elaine, Spring, and Mrs. Carruthers continued to fuss over her, making the final adjustments.

Kim was stunned at how good her sister looked. Despite all the chaos around her, Vicki had pulled it together. Her gown was gorgeous, a high-necked Victorian style, the bodice studded with tiny pearls. Her newly permed hair was tucked back gracefully under her veil, and Elaine stood behind her, holding her train. Kim couldn't believe it. Vicki looked like a princess.

"I feel so spoiled with all of you fussing over me," Vicki said, laughing. "You've all been terrific," she said lightly, hugging Spring and

Elaine. "Especially considering what a basket case I've been," she added with a smile.

Kim grinned, relieved that Vicki's sense of humor had returned. She seemed completely calm now, and for the first time all day, she didn't even ask about the weather.

There was a loud knock on the door, and moments later Miss Phipps came in wearing a pearl-gray suit. In contrast to her frazzled appearance two days earlier at the rehearsal, Miss Phipps looked absolutely in control. She quickly surveyed the bridal party. "Everyone ready?" she said. It was more of a statement than a question.

After Spring and Elaine put the final touches on their makeup, Miss Phipps led them all into a beautifully landscaped private courtyard where the photographer was waiting. They posed beside a flower bed, in the courtyard, beside a birdbath, and next to some stone steps. Kim smiled until her jaw hurt. Then the two mothers in the wedding party arrived, and they took even more photographs.

The sun shone brightly one minute, and then the next it would be covered by a large dark cloud. Vicki didn't seem to notice, but Kim did. And she wasn't alone. Miss Phipps and Kim's mother were also worried, judging by the anxious looks they gave the sky. After a quick, silent plea that it wouldn't rain, Kim crossed her fingers tightly behind her.

When the picture taking was finished, Miss Phipps led everyone back to the hotel suite, then she had a huddled conversation with Kim's mother. "We're going to start in five minutes," Miss Phipps announced. "Please take your places." Kim's heart started to race.

As they waited in the hallway that led down to the garden, Kim's mother came over and drew her aside.

"The wedding's still going to be outside, right?" Kim asked immediately.

"We're going to chance it," her mother replied. She had a faraway look in her eyes. "My baby," she said softly, "you look so pretty today."

"Oh, Mom." Kim blushed.

"I've neglected you terribly because of this wedding," her mother confessed. "You know I didn't mean it, don't you, sweetheart?"

Kim smiled and nodded mutely. She was afraid that if she tried to say a word, she might start crying. After all of Spring's hard work to make her look perfect, the last thing Kim wanted to do was smear all her makeup before the wedding even began.

"I'll make it up to you," her mother promised, giving her a quick peck on the cheek.

"I love you, Mom."

"I love you, too."

Their conversation was interrupted by the sound of the organ. "I've got to get to my seat!" her mother exclaimed. "Good luck, honey. Stand up nice and tall now."

" 'Bye," Kim said, smiling. Somehow, she didn't mind her mother's advice just then. Standing up straight seemed to come naturally to her, part of the new pride she felt in how good she looked.

Miss Phipps herded them up to the top of the stone steps that led down into the garden. Kim looked down at the scene below, and couldn't believe the transformation that had taken place there since the rehearsal.

The gazebo was covered with flowers. White folding chairs, where the guests were now sitting and waiting expectantly, had been set out on the lawn. The classical music that the organist was playing made the setting seem even more romantic. The finishing touch was the pond to the right of the guests, where two swans floated gracefully across the shimmering water.

Then the wedding march began, bringing a lump to Kim's throat. The ushers walked in solemnly, and Kim's eyes flew to Rick in the distance. He looked a little nervous as he brought up the rear, but he was more handsome than ever in his gray cutaway.

"Oh, no," a tiny voice said behind her. Kim glanced back at Vicki, who was looking up at the dark cloud in the sky with her mouth open in dismay. Kim crossed her fingers even tighter. *Don't rain,* she urged silently. *Please!*

Miss Phipps nodded her head, and with a tiny pat, sent Anne down the walkway. The guests turned their heads and gasped at how cute she looked. When the little girl was halfway to the altar, Miss Phipps sent Elaine after her, and then a moment later, Spring slowly followed.

Then it was Kim's turn. At first she felt very nervous because everyone would be looking at her, but once she took her first step, she was relieved to find her feet seemed to move along by themselves. She spotted Joan and Maria in the crowd, and the delight on their faces made her relax even more. She smiled. Then her gaze moved back to the gazebo, and Rick. As she got nearer, she felt him staring at her, too, and she flashed him a brilliant smile.

By the time she reached her place under the gazebo next to Spring, Kim had relaxed completely. She had managed to make it all the way up the aisle with a certain amount of dignity, and she hadn't tripped or stumbled once. She hoped for her mother's sake that she had stood up straight enough, too. Looking over again at

Rick shyly, she noticed that he hadn't taken his eyes off her.

Finally the ceremony began. Even though it was incredibly moving, Kim couldn't keep her mind off Rick. His eyes seemed to be burning into her. Kim's attention was only diverted when Vicki and Max started to say their vows.

When they were pronounced husband and wife, Elaine started sniffling, and Kim blinked back a tear. The look Max and Vicki exchanged before they kissed was something Kim would never forget.

The ceremony was over, and suddenly they were filing out. As Vicki and Max headed back down the aisle, a breeze came up, and a light mist filled the air. Kim had forgotten all about the dark cloud in the excitement of the ceremony but was relieved that it was only mist, and not really rain. Somehow it made the occasion all the more romantic.

She didn't have time to think about that for long, though. Just then Rick appeared in front of her, and they linked arms. They took a couple of steps and then Rick whispered in her ear, "You look so beautiful." Kim melted. She felt as though she were gliding down the path next to him on air.

When they got to the bridge where the rest of the wedding party waited, the mist stopped.

Kim looked over at the pond and thought she saw a rainbow. But when she turned to look again, it was gone. With Rick's strong arm around her shoulders, it didn't matter whether it had been real or not. The day was already magical.

# Chapter Twelve

"Isn't this just lovely?" Kim's grandmother asked her as they entered the hotel ballroom after the ceremony.

Kim nodded mutely. After the pictures of the wedding party had been taken by the pond, she had been separated from Rick in the crowd of well wishers. *Just when things had been so perfect,* Kim thought sadly. But he had been swept away by a group of his own relatives at the same time that her grandparents appeared. She hadn't seen them since they'd arrived, so naturally she had to talk to them first.

"The view is glorious," her grandmother continued, and Kim had to agree. The ballroom's large plate-glass windows overlooked the garden, and she could see the gazebo in the distance.

A bandstand had been set up against the other wall for the orchestra that was going to play after lunch. The dance floor, a wooden deck, was surrounded by tables with exquisite floral arrangements, and Kim noticed with satisfaction that the tablecloths were the exact color of her dress. She craned her neck, looking for Rick. No sign of him anywhere.

Then someone touched her elbow, and Kim whirled around to find Maria and Joan, both looking very excited.

"Hi," Maria exclaimed as she carefully examined Kim's dress. Kim had forgotten that Maria had never seen it. "You look fabulous," Maria said in admiration. "I can't believe you were ever worried that you wouldn't."

"Thanks," Kim said, smiling. "Wasn't the ceremony wonderful?" She really wanted to tell them about Rick, and the looks he had been giving her, but her grandparents were still hovering nearby. "Do you remember my friends Joan and Maria?" she asked her grandparents instead.

Everyone exchanged greetings. Then, to Kim's relief, her father came over and led her grandparents away. "We'll have a long talk later, dear," her grandmother promised before she left.

Maria had an impish expression on her face. "Well," she said, leaning over to whisper in Kim's ear. "Congratulations."

"For what?" Kim asked.

"For how well you did—you didn't trip or anything. You really looked good. In fact, you and Rick were the best-looking couple in the wedding party."

"I guess you must be pretty excited," Joan broke in. "I saw the way he was looking at you."

Kim blushed in spite of herself. "Did you see it, too?" she demanded. "He was making me so nervous I thought I was going to die."

"Well, don't die yet," Maria said, grinning. "Not until I find out if Rick asks you out after the reception."

Kim smiled happily, noticing out of the corner of her eye that people were beginning to take their seats. "I wonder where we're sitting?" she asked casually. She was also wondering where Rick was sitting.

A quick search found the three girls placed together at a table just to the left of the bandstand. To Kim's disappointment, Rick wasn't seated at their table. She looked around nervously.

"Don't worry," Maria said, reading her mind. "He's here somewhere. Just relax."

Kim sighed impatiently. The special feeling

she and Rick had shared during the ceremony seemed to have evaporated the minute it was over. *Have I imagined everything?* Kim wondered. She wished she could find him. One look at his face would tell her everything.

A few minutes later the room settled down, and several white-jacketed waiters appeared with the first course of the luncheon, shrimp cocktail. Kim was taking her first bite when she glimpsed Rick and the best man hurrying into the room. They took seats at a table across the dance floor, directly opposite her.

The minute Rick sat down, Kim saw him looking around the room. *Is he looking for me?* she wondered. Then he saw her, and her question was answered. Their eyes met, and he smiled. Kim smiled back. Her heart started beating double time.

During the rest of the meal Kim tried to keep up with the lively conversation at their table, but all she could think of was Rick, who kept sneaking little peeks at her. Even though he was across the room, his looking at her almost made her feel as though he were there beside her.

After the waiters served the coffee, Max's father went up to the microphone in front of the bandstand to propose a toast. Kim winced, remembering his toast at the family dinner. To her relief, Mr. Wheeler kept his remarks brief and limited them to the bride and groom. Then he introduced the bandleader, a heavyset man with short, slicked-back hair.

"Good afternoon," the bandleader said. "To start off our program this afternoon, I'd like to ask all the members of the wedding party to take the floor."

Everyone started to clap, and Kim got up hesitantly. As she moved to the dance floor, she felt extremely self-conscious—as though she were at a school party hoping someone would ask her to dance, except this time all her relatives were present and watching.

Then, all at once, Rick was at her side. "May I have this dance?" he asked solemnly.

Kim smiled. "Yes, you may," she said equally seriously. The orchestra began to play, and soon they were whirling around the floor with the other members of the wedding party.

At first, Kim felt awkward dancing in front of everyone, and she knew Rick did, too. But as the song continued, they both forgot all about the crowd. It was as though they were in their own private world, dancing to their own private song.

"You're a good dancer," Rick said quietly a few minutes later.

"So are you," Kim replied. It was true, he was

easy to dance with. Finally the song ended, too quickly as far as Kim was concerned, and they stopped and joined in the applause for the orchestra.

Rick leaned over to whisper in her ear. "Can we take a walk somewhere?" he asked shyly.

Kim nodded her head calmly, but her whole body seemed to be churning. Rick took her by the hand and led her off the dance floor to the french doors that led outside. Something in the back of her mind told her they should stay and mingle with the other guests, but Kim didn't care. She had been waiting for that moment far too long to worry about what people might think.

Just as they went through the doors, Kim saw Joan and Maria staring at them in astonishment. Kim managed to shrug her shoulders subtly, as if this kind of thing happened to her all the time. And with a slight smile, she followed Rick outside.

The cloud that had been hovering over the hotel was gone now, and bright sunlight shone over the grounds of the hotel. The grass, still dewy from the mist that had fallen during the ceremony, sparkled in the sun. As Rick led her across the stone path down to the garden, Kim noticed that her pink shoes were getting wet and little pieces of grass were sticking to them. She didn't care.

Rick cleared his throat. "It's been quite a day," he began unsteadily.

"The ceremony was beautiful," Kim agreed.

"It was," he said. "I was surprised. Usually I don't go for that kind of mushy stuff."

"Weddings seem kind of strange to me, too," Kim hedged, trying to say the right thing. "I never really think about them too much." They reached the stone steps leading down to the garden and followed them.

"It's more what they stand for that I like," Rick confessed. "The feeling of family is nice. Everybody's in a good mood and on their best behavior. It's kind of like Christmas in a way. Without the presents, though," he added.

Kim smiled at the comparison. "It's too bad life can't always be like this," she said. They had reached the pond where the two swans were still swimming about aimlessly. As they stood there watching the birds, Kim had the feeling Rick wanted to say something to her—something important, but he just couldn't find the right words.

"I wish we had some bread or something to feed them," he finally said, a faraway look in his eyes.

Kim, lost in her own thoughts, idly wandered over to the gazebo. She paused there, taking in the smell of the flowers. Rick came up beside her. He carefully plucked out a carnation that was woven into the latticework and presented it to her shyly. "For you," he said in a low voice.

In the distance Kim could hear the orchestra playing a waltz. She took the flower he offered shyly and looked into his eyes. They were shining now.

"I was wondering if you'd like to go out with me sometime," Rick said, running his words together very fast. "I'm not very good at this," he added clumsily.

Kim looked down at the lawn. She was sure she was blushing, but she didn't care. "I'm not very good at this kind of thing, either," she admitted, moving her eyes up to meet his. "I'd really like to learn, though."

"Good," he murmured, and then to her complete surprise, he leaned forward and gave her an awkward kiss. Although it was thrilling, it wasn't the kind of thrill that made her want to jump up and down. Instead, she felt a warm glow of happiness spread through her.

They didn't say much after that, strolling around the garden silently for a while. Finally Kim said that they'd better get back to the reception. The way she said it didn't seem forced or nervous, just completely natural.

As they went back up the stairs, Kim noticed that Rick seemed to have something on his mind. Just as they were about to enter the reception hall, he touched her arm. "Would you like to drive down to the ocean and walk on the beach?" he asked.

There was nothing else she'd rather do! But then she realized that she had to answer his question. He stood there expectantly. Finally Kim understood that he wanted to make it a firm date. "Sure," she said. "When?"

"Well," Rick replied, his face breaking into a grin. "How about now?"

It didn't seem as though her heart could pound any faster one more time that day, but it did. "I don't know," Kim said uneasily. Her eyes moved over the room, where the guests were all talking and dancing. *We'd hardly be missed*, she thought.

It didn't take much longer for her to decide. "OK," she agreed, amazed at her daring. "Let me just say goodbye to Vicki."

"Great. I'll meet you in the parking lot in five minutes."

Kim floated across the room to Vicki and, drawing her aside, gave her a big hug and briefly explained about Rick's invitation. Vicki reacted just as she had hoped and told her to go and have a good time. After another more tearful hug, Vicki said she'd call soon, and then Kim broke away, feeling sadder than she had thought she would.

She quickly said goodbye to Maria and Joan, who were taken by the romance of it all, and then to her mother, who didn't seem as pleased.

"Are you sure you want to leave so soon, dear?" she asked Kim uncertainly.

"I'm sure," Kim said.

Kim's eyes must have registered how she felt because her mother yielded gracefully. "Have a good time," she said and gave her daughter a kiss.

Rick was waiting for her in the parking lot, and soon they were driving toward the beach. With the wind whipping through the car windows, it was hard to keep up a conversation, but the looks he shot her said more than any words could.

When they got to the ocean, Rick parked his car in a space right by the boardwalk. "Can you walk on the beach in those?" he asked, looking at her shoes.

"Let me run in there for a second to take off my shoes and stockings," she said, pointing to a cabana just off the boardwalk in the sand.

When she came out, Rick had taken off his shoes and socks and rolled up his pants. As they started toward the ocean, Kim suddenly remembered that Maria had predicted they would end up walking on the beach together. It had seemed so unlikely at the time, she thought. And now it had come true.

When they got to the shoreline, Rick took her hand shyly, and they started to walk down the beach.

A couple of joggers passed them and smiled at their costumes. Kim realized that they were all dressed up, she in her pink dress and Rick in his gray cutaway. It seemed more than romantic. It was a fantasy she'd never dared to imagine.

They continued walking hand in hand, not talking. The beach seemed to go on forever.

We hope you enjoyed reading this book. Some of the titles currently available in the Sweet Dreams series are listed at the front of the book. They are all available at your local bookshop or newsagent, though should you find any difficulty in obtaining the books you would like, you can order direct from the publisher, at the address below. Also, if you would like to know more about the series, or would simply like to tell us what you think of the series, write to:

Kim Prior,
Sweet Dreams,
Transworld Publishers Ltd.,
61–63 Uxbridge Road,
Ealing,
London W5 5SA.

To order books, please list the title(s) you would like, and send together with a cheque or postal order made payable to TRANSWORLD PUBLISHERS LTD. Please allow the cost of the book(s) plus postage and packing charges as follows:

All orders up to a total of £5.00     50p
All orders in excess of £5.00     Free

Please note that payment must be made in pounds sterling; other currencies are unacceptable.

**(The above applies to readers in the UK and Republic of Ireland only)**

If you live in Australia or New Zealand and would like more information about the series, please write to:

Sally Porter,
Sweet Dreams,
Transworld Publishers (Aust) Pty Ltd.
15–23 Helles Avenue
Moorebank
N.S.W. 2170
AUSTRALIA

Kiri Martin,
Sweet Dreams,
c/o Corgi and Bantam Books New Zealand,
Cnr. Moselle and Waipareira Avenues,
Henderson,
Auckland,
NEW ZEALAND

# Kelly Blake
## TEEN MODEL

One day she's an A student at Franklyn High with a major crush on the boy next door. Then she's discovered by the head of the prestigious FLASH! modelling agency. Almost overnight Kelly becomes the hottest new face in the modelling world!

Each of the KELLY BLAKE titles features the ongoing characters and events in Kelly's life. While romance is part of that life, these books are more than romances; they deal with the experiences, conflicts, crises and behind-the-scenes details of modelling.

Ask your bookseller for the titles you have missed:

1. DISCOVERED!
2. RISING STAR
3. HARD TO GET
4. HEADLINERS
5. DOUBLE TROUBLE
6. PARIS NIGHTS

TRUE LOVE! CRUSHES! BREAKUPS! MAKEUPS!

Find out what it's like to be a COUPLE.

Ask your bookseller for any titles you have missed: